COCONUT REPUBLIC

THOMAS J. WOLFENDEN

A POST HILL PRESS BOOK
ISBN: 978-1-61868-809-5
ISBN (eBook): 978-1-61868-808-8

Cover Design by Christian Bentulan

Post Hill
PRESS

Post Hill Press
posthillpress.com

Published in the United States of America

Other books by the author

One Man's Island
One Man's War
Full Moon Fishtown

"History does not long entrust the care of freedom to the weak or the timid."

DWIGHT D. EISENHOWER, inaugural address,
Jan. 20, 1953

"It is not the critic who counts; not the man who points out how the strong man stumbles, or where the doer of deeds could have done them better. The credit belongs to the man who is actually in the arena, whose face is marred by dust and sweat and blood; who strives valiantly; who errs, who comes short again and again, because there is no effort without error and shortcoming; but who does actually strive to do the deeds; who knows great enthusiasms, the great devotions; who spends himself in a worthy cause; who at the best knows in the end the triumph of high achievement, and who at the worst, if he fails, at least fails while daring greatly, so that his place shall never be with those cold and timid souls who neither know victory nor defeat."

THEODORE ROOSEVELT, "Citizenship in a Republic" Paris,
France April 23, 1910

"People sleep peaceably in their beds at night only because rough men stand ready to do violence on their behalf."

GEORGE ORWELL

CHAPTER 1

Belize, October, 1986

It wasn't quite 9AM and the temperature was rapidly climbing as the hot equatorial sun beat down on them from a cloudless sky. The steam from the thick jungle that kissed the beach rolled out to engulf them, and the slight sea breeze coming off the Gulf of Mexico did little to cool the two travelers.

They approached a fisherman who was busy tending his gill nets at the high tide mark, and showed him a photograph. The man nodded, pointing to a grass shack with a thatched roof ringed with coconut palms nestled inside the jungle.

Although there were no signs of life, there was a rusted old Jeep CJ parked next to the shack, which told them someone must be at home. They thanked the fisherman and plodded off into the soft snow-white sand toward the hut. When they got nearer, they could see that it had no front wall, and the open interior led onto a thatched veranda that faced the ocean.

There was a canvas hammock strung between two thick bamboo posts in the opening, and as they neared the veranda, the larger of the two oddly dressed men stepped onto the short flight of steps leading up. The floor was littered with empty beer bottles and women's clothing, and there was a battered galvanized steel Eskimo cooler near one end that was leaking water.

"Hello? Captain Kruger?" the man in the lead called out.

A woman's head popped into view from the hammock. She was dark-skinned with mussed, long black hair, and must have had some Mayan or Aztec blood in her. *"Qué?"* she said, yawning.

"Hola! Captain Kruger?" the second one asked with a smile.

"Sí," she said and nudged the lump next to her. *"Señor* Dan."

"What?" came the grumbled reply and a large man appeared from the hanging bed. He was darkly tanned and his thick mop of unkempt, longish, blond hair was a deep contrast. He pushed the woman out of the bed and sat up. She fell to the floor and scrambled to retrieve her clothing, trying unsuccessfully to cover her naked body from the now wide-eyed strangers.

She let out a stream of abuse in Spanish towards the blond-haired man in the hammock as she ran out through a back passage they hadn't noticed. He picked up a half-full bottle of beer from under the hammock and threw it haphazardly at her retreating form.

"Vamonos!" he said, facing his visitors, smiled sheepishly, and said, "She'll be back. She always comes back. Now what can I do for you two?"

"You are Captain Daniel Kruger?" the larger of the two said in an accent that Kruger wasn't familiar with.

His eyes narrowed to slits as he studied his two unwanted visitors, his gaze boring holes through them. He let the stare continue for several more seconds. "I haven't been called that in quite a while. Who are you two? You're too uptight to be Agency," he said, sitting up, his tanned legs dangling down.

He reached into the cooler, pleasantly surprised to find there was still some ice left. He scooped up some cold water and threw it on his face, then grabbed a bottle of Dos Equis and popped the top. Taking a long pull from the bottle, he took stock of his uninvited guests.

The fat one with the bad comb over was a Doppelgänger of Zero Mostel, and the shorter one reminded him of Arte

Johnson. He could clearly see neither was used to the heat, and the sweat was ruining what appeared to be quite expensive Italian suits. He immediately named them Tweedle Dee and Tweedle Dumb in his mind.

"Captain Kruger, my name is Nils Van Die Kaap, and my associate here is Jon Bruhl," the larger of the two said. "We represent a South African mining corporation, and we've come to offer you employment."

"South Africa, huh? I was wondering where your accent was from. And you've come to offer me employment? That's interesting. Tell me more," he said, fixing them with an ice-cold stare that unnerved both visitors.

"First we must ask," said the shorter of the two sweating men, "you are indeed Daniel Kruger, born September 12, 1946? You went to Scranton University? Enlisted in the US Army in 1967? Commissioned on the Battlefield in Vietnam? Served with the 5th Special Forces Group?"

"Yeah, yeah, that's me," Kruger said dismissively, waving the beer bottle at them.

"Recruited by the Central Intelligence Agency in 1973?"

"Spare me the bio. That's me. How the fuck did you get that? No one—and I mean *no one*—knew I went to work for them."

"You did, did you not?" the man asked. He wiped his sweat soaked face with a handkerchief, placed it back in his pocket and continued. "Like my colleague stated, we've come to offer you a job."

"I may have worked for them, or maybe I'm a burned out *Encyclopedia Britannica* salesman. And what makes you think I need a job?" he said, finishing off his beer and opening another one.

"Isn't it a little early for drinking, Captain Kruger?" Van Die Kaap asked.

"Captain, you have $187.32 in your bank account," the shorter one cut in before he could reply. "You are six months behind on your rent here in this lovely little cottage. I think you will need employment soon."

Kruger was silent for a moment, taking in what he'd been told. Yeah, he was almost flat broke. José was a good landlord, but he was getting itchy for his rent. He would need to make some money here shortly. He took another long pull from the beer, fumbled in the hammock, and pulled out a crumpled pack of Marlboros. Opening the pack, he pulled out several broken ones, and one by one, tossed them carelessly on the floor. When he found an unbroken cigarette, he lit it with an ancient and scarred Zippo lighter. He took a deep drag, looked right at the two sweating men and blew out a large cloud of smoke, scratching his five days' growth of stubble.

"Who the fuck are you people, anyway? You come traipsing in here and know all kinds of things about me, I don't know dick about you two," he said, irritated with the intrusion.

The taller of the two said, "Captain, like we said, we represent a large South African mining company, and we're in need of someone with your, how should I say it? *Expertise?*"

"Expertise, huh? And how did you find out all this stuff about me? *That* I don't like, not one little bit." Kruger took another drag of his cigarette.

"We like to do research on the people on whom we wish to employ, make sure our money is well spent. Your record is quite impressive, to say the least." The short one set down his briefcase and held his hands out, as if pleading.

"Alright, you've piqued my interest. What type of job are you talking about?" Kruger asked.

"We are offering you a security job," the nearer one said. "We need you to head a small security detail, dignitary protection."

"Bodyguards, huh? Where would this be?"

"Korotonga."

"Where the hell is that?" Kruger snapped, dropping his cigarette butt into the empty beer bottle. "It doesn't sound like Africa to me. Then again, countries there change their names more times than a woman changes her mind."

He stood, and for the first time the men realized he was naked. Kruger walked over unabashedly to the railing of the veranda and relieved himself, his six-foot, two-inch frame towering over both of the other men.

"Korotonga is a small island nation in the South Pacific, northwest of Fiji. It is halfway between there and the Solomon Islands," Bruhl said.

"So why does this place need a security detail?" Kruger asked skeptically, facing them.

"After they gained their independence from the United Kingdom in 1965, there have been several coups, and recently there's been another attempt. The current president is in fear for his life and we've had a... 'special' relationship with him, and it is in our best interests that he remains in power."

"May I ask what that 'special relationship' is?"

"No you may not," Van Die Kaap said.

"Captain Kruger, we have a large phosphate mine on the island. The sitting president there and our company have a very...lucrative arrangement for the mining, transport, and shipping of the product. We at Amalgamated Phosphates would like to ensure this ongoing relationship," Bruhl explained.

"Phosphate mine, huh? Doesn't this guy have an army?"

"He does, and they're quite loyal to him..."

"He doesn't quite trust them enough," Kruger finished. "All right, if it's only a protection detail, I can deal with that. How many men and do you need me to recruit them?"

"No, we already have men in place. We need you to lead them."

"Are they locals?"

"No, no indigenous personnel. The president was quite adamant about that. They are all like you, professional soldiers from around the world."

"Like me?" Kruger grinned. *No, there's no one quite like me,* he thought. "Why not use ex-South African or Rhodesian Army vets?"

"It is the nature of those men that they wouldn't do it on principle, Captain," Van Die Kaap said a little uncomfortably.

"You mean they won't take orders from a black man? Isn't that right, Mister Van Die Clap?"

"It is Van Die *Kaap,* and quite frankly, yes, that is our problem there," Van Die Kaap said with some exasperation.

"I kind of figured that. Now let's talk money," Kruger said, not liking these two at all, politics aside. However, he did need the money so he was willing to walk the razor's edge for a time, even if it was only to keep him in beer and nachos.

"We are prepared to pay you a fifty thousand dollar advance, in addition to a ten thousand dollar per month salary," Bruhl said.

Although Kruger was stunned, he didn't show it. That was a lot of money, a lot more money than he'd ever heard any mercenary being paid before. The thought hit him then. Was that what he was turning into? A mercenary? Then the sadistic streak in him showed and he decided to play with them a little. He stood there in the middle of his hut and looked at the two men with his piercing, gunmetal gray eyes for several moments without saying a word, letting the pause drag out to the point it was becoming unbearable to his visitors.

"Make it one hundred thousand dollars up front and twenty thousand a month," he said flatly, waiting for the refusal.

He was shocked when Van Die Kaap said, "Done. That will be acceptable."

"I guess your company doesn't offer medical, dental, and eyeglass coverage?"

"No sir, we do not," Bruhl said, missing the sarcasm completely.

"Can I have a day or two to think about it?"

"Absolutely not," Van Die Kaap said. "We need your answer before we depart."

"Kind of putting me on the spot, you know. It's a big decision to make at the drop of a hat."

"We must know now," Bruhl said firmly.

"Alright then, you have a deal, and a new chief of security," Kruger said, pulling on a pair of cut-off shorts, much to the relief of his guests. "How do I get there?"

"We have your travel arrangements right here," Bruhl said. He opened his briefcase, pulled out a folder, and handed it to him. Kruger took it and shuffled through the papers, inspecting the airline tickets and boarding passes in his name already printed out.

Nice, they were flying him first class.

He looked at them over the top of the envelope with a raised eyebrow. "You were pretty sure of yourselves, huh?"

Van Die Kaap pulled out another, larger manila envelope and handed it to him, ignoring his last question. "These are the dossiers of the men you will be in charge of, and some other pertinent information you may find helpful."

Kruger walked over to a table and hunted through some papers until he found a pen and writing tablet. He took them and wrote something down, tore off the page, and handed it to Bruhl. "That's the number to a bank account in the Cayman Islands. Wire the money into that account, the first one hundred grand today, and monthly payments on the first of each month for the monthly twenty grand. If the first hundred isn't in there by the time my flight leaves..." he looked at the papers they gave him, "the day after tomorrow, I won't be on the plane, got that?"

"Captain Kruger, the money will be there by the end of business hours today," Bruhl said.

"Alright then, we have a deal. I have one final question."

"Yes, Captain Kruger?"

"I'm not going over there to fight some little bush war, not going to be part of any coup?" he asked, opening his third beer of the morning and looking at them skeptically, wondering what it was they were setting him up for. That was a shitpot of money they were throwing at him. It must be a lucrative phosphate mine indeed. "Because, gentlemen, if it is, I pull the plug immediately. I've had my fill of those and I will be greatly upset if I'm being set up."

"Let me reassure you, Captain Kruger, it is purely a presidential security detail."

"You've got yourselves a new employee. Who do I contact in case of a problem?"

"Here is my card, Captain," Van Die Kaap said, pulling out a business card holder and offering one to him. Kruger took it and looked at it briefly, tossing it on the table. Van Die Kaap held out his hand and Kruger took it, giving him a bone-crushing grip.

"Believe me, if there are any problems, I will be in touch with you," he said, looking him dead in the eye. The man cowed, looking away reflexively.

"Then I will bid you a good day, sir," Van Die Kaap said, and the visitors took their leave, wandering back down the beach the way they'd come.

Dan walked back out on the veranda and sat down with his beer on the front steps and watched them disappear down the beach. He took a sip of his beer, his mind churning. Looking out toward the sea, he saw a large sailing yacht scud by, not a hundred yards from the surf, wondering what in the hell he'd gotten himself into.

The fact that they knew everything about him, things that should never have seen the light of day, must mean it was some hell of a big corporation to dig up that stuff. And they found him so easily, simply walked right up the beach to his hut.

Well, he wasn't exactly hiding. He could have used several of the 'legends' he had from his days at the CIA, and one he made for himself that even the Agency didn't know about. In hindsight, however, it wouldn't have mattered. Apparently they had enough juice to find out about anything. He laughed at how he had given them his bank information. They already had his balance, so they probably already knew the account details.

"Well I'll be. Three hundred and forty grand a year to protect some president? I bet the Secret Service doesn't get paid like that!" he said aloud. As he stubbed out his cigarette, a black and white cat crawled out from underneath the hut and curled around his legs.

"What do you think of that, El Gato?" he said, scratching the cat behind the ears. "Let's get you fed."

Dan stood and went back inside, followed by the cat. He went to the cupboard and retrieved a can of tuna, opened it, and set in on the plank floor. The cat dug into the fish with gusto and he looked down at it with a smile. He then glanced around his place with chagrin. It wasn't much, but it sort of kept the rain off his head. He picked up an only slightly soiled tank top off the floor and threw that on, grabbed his wallet and checkbook, plopped a battered Philadelphia Phillies ball cap on his head, and headed out to the Jeep.

He started the vehicle with the keys he'd always leave in the ignition; he was too far away from anywhere except a few fishermen's huts here and there to ever worry about someone stealing it. It was what he loved about this place. He put the jeep into gear, and the cat jumped up on his lap, meowing loudly.

"*Señor* Gato, you cannot come with me. Stay here and guard the hut," he said, and tossed the cat onto the ground. Pulling around to a narrow dirt track cut into the jungle, he headed off toward town, the branches and vines scraping the sides as he bounced along the rutted road. His mind was spinning at this point. That was a lot of money for some security puke. And the way those two headhunters came strolling up the beach? That was different.

But the money. That was a lot of money to be had. That was what had finally hooked him. The last time he saw money thrown around like that, it was for another product coming out of Columbia that was quite popular now in the States, and it wasn't the coffee.

It had better not be anything to do with that, or he'd be angry. He'd had his fill of the sneaky, fucked up games the Agency was playing down there, and it was why he had pulled the plug a year ago. Too many times he'd seen the Agency propping up one tin pot dictator so they could fuck another tin pot dictator, and used the proceeds of drugs to do it all in the name of Foreign Policy and fighting the Cold War against Communism.

He was sick of it. No one had principles anymore. And that was the one thing they could never strip him of. He did need the money, so he'd do this job, maybe a year or so, then quietly retire back here in Belize and he could live his life in quiet obscurity where a little money would go a long, long way.

The jungle track led out to a paved, two-lane blacktop road and he pulled out, turning left to head toward the town of San Christos, ten miles south. He pushed the vehicle up to fifty miles an hour, as fast as the old Jeep and potholed road would allow. The cool wind felt good on his skin, and was welcome after the sweltering heat of the jungle.

He popped a cassette tape into his stereo and was welcomed by some cool riffs from The Eagles. He drove down the highway past huts and tin shacks, and several locals waved, recognizing the big Gringo. He smiled and waved back, happy to be somewhere that he felt at home.

As he neared town, he saw more and more people, and makeshift fruit and vegetable stands set up along the road, where the locals sold fresh bananas, mangoes, coconuts, papayas, and pineapples to passersby. He pulled up in front of a huge two-story concrete building with a faux-stone façade. It was the Royal Excelsior Hotel, built in the British Colonial fashion in 1901, owned by a German expatriate with a dubious past, and Dan had the sneaking suspicion that past included a black uniform with skull and crossbones 'Death's head' and 'SS' collar insignia, although he never asked. No one did here, and no one cared. Yet another reason why he liked it so much; the quiet anonymity that was so attractive. No one knew his past, and no one asked. For all anyone knew here, he was another American expatriate beach bum living off a trust fund that Daddy had set up.

He took a quick look around, then glanced up to the cloudless sky and wondered if it would rain today. He shut the Jeep off and exited the vehicle, walking barefoot through the open double doors to the hotel. He walked across the worn carpet of the empty lobby into the dimly lit pub and up to the bar. There were a few other patrons sitting at tables, but they ignored him, which was fine and dandy to Dan anyway. A large, round jovial man emerged from a back room with a big toothy grin and came up to Dan.

"Ah! *Guten tag*, Herr Kruger!"

"And a good day to you also, Franz," Dan said, replying in English. Dan spoke German like a native and was also fluent in Russian and Spanish, though never, ever let on to the proprietor that he did. He liked the illusion of being merely another ignorant American, and it also gave him the opportunity to eavesdrop openly on Franz's phone calls from time to time, although that never gleaned any juicy information he could use. Still, it kept him in practice with his field craft.

"What shall I get for you today, Herr Kruger?"

"I'll have a Dos Equis, Franz," he said, looking around the place again.

"Are you sure you would not like to try the house brew, Herr Kruger?" Franz asked with a big grin.

"Thank you, Franz, I'll have a Dos Equis," Dan said diplomatically.

Franz fancied himself a master brewer, and brewed his own beer in small batches. He called it *Das Alt Housbrau Bier.* After trying it for the first time a year prior, Dan called it *Alt Hundpissen Bier* or 'old dog piss,' and stayed as far away from it as he could.

"Have you seen José?"

"No, have not seen him today. However, it is early yet," Franz said, pulling a cold bottle of beer out of the cooler and popping the top. "Will this be on your tab?"

"I'll be paying my tab in full today, Franz."

"That is good news indeed," he said, placing the bottle in front of Dan and smiling broadly. Dan owed Franz quite a bit of money. He wasn't so pushy yet as to call in the markers, but if Dan didn't settle up his bills soon, he would be less than welcome in the hotel's bar, or anyplace else in town.

"Yes, it is good news," he said, taking a pull off the beer. "I've had a very interesting morning."

"And I should say you had an interesting evening with Maria," Franz said with a hearty laugh and a wink.

"Franz, look, I'll be going away for a bit, and want to pay up all my debts before I go."

"That is very good news indeed! You are not in trouble of any sort?" he asked, getting a cross look on his face.

Dan laughed. "No, nothing like that. I got a job and it's overseas. I'll be gone for a while, not sure how long. Just want to tidy up loose ends before I go."

"What is it you will be doing?" Franz asked, placing an ashtray on the bar in front of Dan when he produced his cigarettes and lighter. Dan pulled a Marlboro out of his pack and tamped it on the Zippo, put in to his lips and lit it, then took a sip of beer.

"Consulting work," Dan said noncommittally.

"Oh, is that what you do? You are a consultant. I have always wondered what it was that you do." Franz eyed the Zippo lighter. Dan quickly saw what he was looking at, the battered and scratched Zippo he carried had the Special Forces crest on it, *De Oppresso Libre*, or Free the Oppressed, on a scroll underneath in Latin. He palmed it and put it in his pocket nonchalantly.

"Yes, I'm a consultant. I consult on things."

Franz asked, "You were in the military of some sort then, Herr Kruger?"

"What? Oh, the lighter? Boy Scouts."

"They let you smoke cigarettes in the Boy Scouts?"

"We start young in the States. Be prepared and all that shit."

"If you say so, Herr Kruger." Franz let out a huge belly-laugh and walked away shaking his head, leaving Dan to himself. He stood there for a few moments, contemplating his situation and began having second thoughts. Had he made the right decision? It was kind of quick; he didn't know those two jokers from bar of soap, but he needed the money.

So you become a mercenary, eh, Danny boy?

South African phosphate mine indeed. They'd caught him at the right time when he wasn't prepared to even make the quick, decisive choices, he didn't have the time to sit down and think about it. Were they playing him? He hoped not, for their sake. Because if they were...

He let that dark though leave his mind as quickly as it came. He stubbed out his cigarette and taking his beer, walked over to an ancient phone booth near the rear of the bar. He pushed open the folding door and entered, taking a seat on a wooden stool built into the side. He picked up the receiver and dialed the international toll-free number from memory. He had a photographic memory, especially with numbers. He could see, or be told any number, and be able to recall it at any time, sometimes years later.

After a few rings, a woman with a Caribbean accent answered, and after giving the proper numbers and password to ensure he was who he said he was, he got the answer he was hoping for. He thanked the woman and hung up, then let out a long whistle. Exiting out of the booth, he headed back to the bar. Setting his beer down, he pulled out his checkbook from his back pocket and wrote out a check for what he figured he owed Franz, plus a little extra. Tearing the check out, he laid it on the bar next to his cigarettes and beer, thinking those two *Saffers* must have worked fast to get the money into his account that quickly. He took another long pull off his beer and wrote out another check to his landlord.

Franz came back out from the back room and Dan motioned him over and handed him the check. "There, that should cover what I owe you, plus a little extra."

Franz picked up the check and his eyes grew wide when he saw the amount. "*Ach du lieber! Ja*, this will be more than enough, Herr Kruger!"

"Here's the back rent I owe José, plus six months' advance rent," Dan said, handing him that check as well. "Please be sure he gets that."

"I will! I will! This 'consulting' you do must be quite lucrative, Herr Kruger," Franz said as he reached into the cooler for another beer, which he sat in front of Dan, winking and smiling broadly.

"It keeps me in beer and chips, Franz."

"And, these checks, how do you say it? They are not made of rubber?" Franz asked skeptically.

Dan laughed. "No, Franz, they won't bounce."

"That is good!"

"I need to ask a favor."

"Yes?"

"I'd like a room here for two nights, and I'll need a ride to the airport," Dan requested.

"Done. I will drive you there myself, and you can keep your Jeep behind the hotel until you return."

"Thank you. I have to go back to my place and get a few things and I'll come back later."

"I will have a room ready for you upon your return," Franz promised.

It was at that moment Dan was hit hard with the image of John Banner, playing Sergeant Shultz in *Hogan's Heroes* and he smiled to himself. That was exactly who Franz looked like to Dan.

"That would be perfect," Dan said, picking up his things and heading back out to his Jeep. He hopped in, started it, and held the cold bottle of beer on his forehead for a moment, savoring the coolness, then he put the Jeep into gear, backed out onto the street, and headed back towards his hut on the beach. He took a long pull off the bottle and tossed in the rear of the Jeep as he sped off down the potholed road. Once there, he parked the Jeep and was greeted by the cat, who immediately hopped up onto the hood of the vehicle and curled up into a little fur ball.

He walked up the wooden steps, stepped into his hut and, with hands on his hips took stock of his home. A far cry from the Post-War Cape Cod style home he lived in with his parents and sister in Scranton, Pennsylvania so many years ago. That life, the old, carefree Dan Kruger, was long gone, and he could never get those years back. He let the melancholy thoughts drift to the back of his mind and got to the task at hand.

With not many possessions to begin with, he didn't have much to pack. He quickly gathered some items—shoes, a pair of US Army-issued jungle boots, two sets of old and battered OG-107 slant-pocket jungle fatigues, and his toiletry kit. He packed them into a battered American Tourister suitcase. He felt the lining of the suitcase and pulled it out some, exposing a hidden pocket where he kept a number of false passports from various European countries in his 'Legend' name, and made sure the dates were all still valid.

He replaced them and resealed the lining then found his real passport, and after checking to make sure that also was still valid, pocketed it. He looked around, scanning to see if he forgot anything. The place would be okay left alone for a while, and El Gato would be fine. Maria would come and take care of things in his absence. The last thing he did was go to the cupboard and retrieve a large coffee can. He pulled out a Browning Hi-Power 9mm pistol and extra magazine he'd kept hidden there, covered with his old Green Beret. The pistol he placed in his suitcase under his underwear. He looked at the beret, the 5th Special Forces Flash and Captain's bars still shining, and tossed that into the suitcase also. He was rapidly going from the mindset of beach bum to soldier again, and was mission focused now, whatever the mission was.

Security, he told himself. That's what the mission is, keeping some president alive.

That's all he needed to do and make well over a cool quarter of a million a year. It would be easy.

There were little warning buzzers starting to go off in the back of his mind. He pushed them away, ignoring them in return for thoughts of a very nice payday. He figured he'd do this one job, come back here, buy the place from José, and build a nice cabana with running water and electricity, and live out the rest of his life in quiet obscurity.

He tossed his suitcase into the back of the Jeep and took one final look around. He climbed back into the Jeep and headed back off down the rutted road through the jungle again, back towards town. He thought of the hot shower and the nice clean sheets in the hotel room and smiled. Living out here was nice for its isolation, although it did lack some things he sometimes missed. He'd stay at the hotel for the next two nights, get cleaned up, have a hot shower, shave, and haircut. He drove around to the back of the hotel and parked in the rear. Retrieving his suitcase, he took the keys and walked in through the rear entrance that led directly into the rear of the hotel's bar. He noticed that there were a few more British tourists in the place now and ignored them as he stepped back up to the bar. Lighting a cigarette, he saw Franz step back out. The jovial German smiled and came over, offering him a key.

"Herr Kruger. Here is the key to the best room in the hotel."

"That wasn't necessary, Franz," Dan said.

"*Och*! Yes, it is!"

"Okay, thanks," Dan said, looking at the fob for the room number. Taking his suitcase, he left Franz to tend to his other customers and walked out to the lobby, where a pair of ancient Otis elevators stood waiting. He hit the 'Up' button and the doors immediately opened. He entered and hit '5' and the doors shut. He rode up and the doors opened into a Spartan hallway and Dan was slapped in the face by a wall of hot, humid air. He immediately broke out into a sweat as he stepped out and followed the numbers to his room. Unlocking the door, he opened it to be rewarded by a blast of cool air.

Franz must have told the staff to turn on the room's air conditioner before he arrived. The un-air conditioned hallway was a sauna and this was a welcome relief. He entered, locked the door behind him, tossed his suitcase on the queen-size bed, and looked around. It was decorated in Art-Deco style and looked like it hadn't been used since the 1940s. It was clean and cool, and that's all that mattered to him.

He stripped naked and taking his toiletry kit, went to the bathroom where he found an equally old, thankfully clean bathroom. He turned on the taps to the shower and soon the room was filled with steam. He showered, toweled off, and wiped the mist from the mirror. Looking at his reflection for a moment, he pondered his new job. He hoped it would be an easy one, but for some nagging reason, he doubted it now. What had seemed easy a few hours ago now left him with nagging questions he couldn't answer.

Too late to go back.

He quickly shaved and went out into the main room where he found a small refrigerator, which he found that Franz had stocked with Dos Equis beer for him. Taking a bottle, he twisted off the cap and took a large pull. He took out the larger of the two manila envelopes from his suitcase, tossed that on the bed, then fished out the pistol and loaded it, racking a round into the chamber and placing the safety on. He sat down on the bed, contents on his lap. He lit a cigarette, then began reading about Korotonga.

The South Africans were quite thorough, going so far as to make everything in miles instead of kilometers, which was totally unnecessary. Ever since the formation of NATO, everything in the US Military was in metric so everything would be interchangeable with other NATO allies, so he was quite well-versed in the metric system and could do the conversions in his head. Flipping over the cover page, he saw that the Republic of Korotonga consisted of three islands, the main one being roughly 2/3 the size of Viti Levu in Fiji. It was 60 miles long, 44 miles wide, and 4,328 square miles in area. The other two islands in the group were Korotona, only four square miles in area and sat a half mile off the main port and city of Kotara, the nation's capital, and was uninhabited. Koromomo, also uninhabited, sat several miles to the north and was basically a mud flat.

It had a population of roughly 50,000, one-third of which was of East Indian descent, brought to the island by the British before the First World War to harvest sugar cane. The rest were indigenous islanders, closely related to the Fijians. It was a British Crown Colony until 1965, when it gained its independence. During World War II, it was occupied by the Japanese after overrunning the British garrison, although no major conflicts were reported.

The island had been 'hopped over' by the advancing allied troops, and the Japanese garrison was left to starve through lack of supplies when the sea routes from Japan were cut off by the advancing Allied armies and US submarines.

Dan put down the folder, lit another cigarette and took a pull from his beer. He blew out a cloud of smoke. The damn thing read like a CIA fact book.

He skimmed through the rest before putting it down. He'd save it for the flight out. He knew that would be a long one, even in first class. Thankfully, it wouldn't be in the cargo hold of a C-141 or C-130. That truly would be an unpleasant flight. He stubbed out his cigarette and went to the fridge to get another beer when there was a tap on the door. He picked up the pistol, and grabbing the towel he'd used to dry off earlier off the floor, he wrapped it around his still naked waist and walked over to the door, peering through the peephole. He saw Maria standing there sheepishly, looking around as if she hoped no one would see her. He grinned and opened the door. She smiled when she saw him.

"*Señor* Dan, are you not angry with me no more?"

"No, I never was angry at you. Please, come in," he said, standing aside as she breezed by him into the center of the room.

"*Señor* Franz tell me you were here."

"I'm glad," he said, shutting the door and locking it, dropping the towel with a smile. He placed the pistol on the nightstand, took her slight frame in his arms, and kissed her deeply, pulling her towards the bed. He picked her up as if she was light as a feather and tossed her playfully on the bed.

Maria was tiny in comparison to Dan. She stood barely five-foot-tall in bare feet, and Dan's six-foot-two frame towered over her. She pulled off her sundress with a quick motion and rolled on top of him. They made love with the late afternoon sunlight streaming in the window, and the only sounds were their breathing and the old Cold Point air conditioner working overtime to battle the heat and humidity. When they were done, Dan laid back with his head propped up on the pillows, Maria's head on his chest. He ran his fingers through her soft, long hair. They lay like that for quite a while.

"*Señor* Dan, are you a dangerous man?"

"Why do you ask that?"

"*La pistola*," she said, pointing at his handgun.

"It's insurance."

"I know dangerous people before. Some good dangerous, some bad dangerous."

"I'm only dangerous to people who piss me off."

"I saw men like you before," Maria said. "In my village."

"Am I good dangerous or bad dangerous?" he asked with a smile, however, the look on her face wiped it away.

"I think you can be both, *ti amo*," she said flatly.

"I'd like to think I was one of the good guys."

"I believe you are, *Señor* Dan. You can be hard sometimes also. I see it in your eyes."

"You do?"

"*Sí*. I see it deep down. You would do great harm to people who cross you. Franz and José do not see it, I do."

"Are you afraid of me?" he asked, stroking her bare back.

"No, I am not afraid of you. Men like you help teach my villagers to be soldiers to fight the Sandinistas who kill my family. It is why I run away to here to find work."

"Will you want to go back to Nicaragua some day?"

"*Sí*, when the fighting is done. Maybe someday you will come with me?"

"I was there once. Your countrymen didn't like me and my friends."

"When the fighting is over, it will be *mucho mejor*, much better, no?"

"Yes, I do believe it will. *Viva La Contra!*" he said and kissed the top of her head.

"I do know this. I do know that I would not want to be your enemy, *Señor* Dan."

"Is that so?"

"*Sí. Señor* Franz thinks you are some rich *Americano*. I know better. He tells me you go for job overseas now. You go and teach others to fight for their freedom like you do in Nicaragua?"

"No, Maria. It's a consulting job. I don't do that anymore. I left that life far behind me," Dan said without a lot of conviction.

"I ask again, *ti amo*, why *la pistola*?" Maria asked in a frightened voice.

"Because carrying around a whole cop would be a pain in the ass."

"You are funny sometimes." She giggled and pinched one of his nipples.

"Yeah, I've been told that before. I'm a funny guy. Maria, please keep all of this to yourself, okay? The pistol, and my past."

"I do not tell *Señor* Franz anything. It is plain to see what it is, and if he is too *estúpido* to see what is before his eyes..."

Dan kissed her head again. "Maria, I gave up that life. Too much deception and too many lies. I want to grow old with all my bits in one piece."

"*Sí!* And I like your bits!"

"Oh, you do, do you?" he said, pinching her butt and she squealed.

"I am serious. I want you to grow old also."

"Will you take care of El Gato for me?"

"Does that mean you will be back?" she asked, spinning around to face him and resting her head on her hand.

"*Sí.* Yes, I will be back. I don't know when, maybe a year or so, but I will be back."

"Then yes, I will take care of El Gato and make a nice home for you for when you return." She began to kiss his chest all over.

Dan looked up to the ceiling and moaned softly, wondering what in the world he was doing. Was he deceiving Maria too?

It was a security job, nothing more. And hopefully it would only last a year and he could come back and live a nice quiet life. He really liked Maria. While he wasn't sure he loved her, he enjoyed her company, and her pleasant diversions.

How long had it been since he'd had a serious relationship with any woman? Too far back to remember, and working for the Agency wasn't exactly the chick magnet that Hollywood led one to believe. He was no James Bond, bedding every hot property he met. Being a field agent for the Central Intelligence Agency was like being a soldier. Although there were no medals or parades, not that he got a warm welcome home from Vietnam, the only thing one would get for a job well done or job disaster would be an unmarked grave somewhere in some Central American jungle and a posthumous gold star on a wall at CIA Headquarters in Langley, Virginia that only other CIA pukes would ever see. Nothing much to illicit warm and fuzzy feelings, and definitely no chick magnet Bond stuff.

"I do not like the fighting, *Señor* Dan. Sandinistas killed my family and now all I have is you," Maria said.

"No fighting, Maria. And I will be back."

"Do you promise me?"

"*Sí*. I promise. I want to buy the place from José and we'll build a nice villa on the property."

"And we will have a boat?" she asked, biting his nipple playfully.

"Yes, we'll buy a boat and take rich *Americanos* and Brits fishing, Maria," he said breathlessly.

"That will be the life for us then, no?"

"*Sí*, that will be the life for us, no fighting, no wars. Fun in the sun, and fishing every day."

"Los niños?"

Sí, y los niños, mi amor." He wondered if he meant it.

He rolled on top of her and kissed her deeply. Maria reached over to the bedside lamp and switched it off, forgotten for now his upcoming journey.

CHAPTER 2

The next two days passed quickly and were a pleasant diversion. Maria's company kept Dan pleasantly preoccupied and left little time for him to think about his new job. Well rested and fed by Franz's wife, who was an excellent cook, Dan now stood in the lobby dressed in casual khaki Dockers and a button-down shirt and tie. The new haircut that Maria had given him gave him the look of a well-travelled conservative businessman as opposed to the aging beach-bum look he'd sported a few days ago. Maria stood holding his hand as Franz emerged from behind the reception desk.

"Ah, I see you are ready. We will leave immediately!"

Dan turned to Maria and kissed her deeply. "Goodbye, Maria. Take good care of El Gato," he said, not wanting to say anything more. He hated goodbyes.

Maria's eyes filled with tears. "*Sí.* I will take good care of him. *Via con Dios.*"

"*Via con Dios,*" he said then turned to Franz. "Let's go."

Dan picked up his suitcase and walked with Franz out through the lobby and to his massive Mercedes that was sitting at the curb, engine running and air conditioner on high. Franz popped the trunk and Dan put his old, battered suitcase in, and walked to the passenger side, getting in. As they started off down the road, he chanced one last look back, only to see Maria standing on the sidewalk in front of the hotel weeping into her hands. He looked away rapidly, though not soon enough to not have the image seared into his memory.

He hated this, and maybe it was why he never had someone serious in his life. It was almost twenty years ago, and the memory of his mother standing at the front door to his house in Scranton crying unabashedly as the Yellow Cab took him away to the airport for basic training in the Army was still fresh in his mind. Every time he thought of it, it tore a little bit more of his heart out.

He cracked the window slightly and lit a cigarette as Franz barreled down the road, driving the huge car as if he was the vanguard Panzer, rolling through France in the Blitzkrieg. The big car gave a rather pleasant ride despite the poor condition of the road.

"Thank you again, Franz."

"It is no trouble at all, Herr Kruger. Besides, it gives me an excuse to get away from Hilda for a day," Franz laughed.

"You'll hold my mail?" Dan asked, flicking an ash out the window.

"*Ja*, I will hold your mail for you," Franz replied. "When does your flight depart?"

"Noon."

"*Och*. We will have ample time to get there. Belize City is only one hour away."

"As long as we get there in one piece, Franz."

Franz passed an overcrowded bus at what felt like 80 miles an hour. He let out a huge belly laugh as he careened down the road in the direction of the airport. "So, tell me. This 'Boy Scouts'. Much interesting things to do there?"

"Yeah, interesting stuff to do. Not that I do anything like that anymore," Dan replied, knowing that Franz was now on a fishing expedition.

"I was once in the Boy Scouts also, many, many years ago," Franz said with a certain reserved pride.

Hitler Youth? Dan thought with a little grin. "I kind of figured as much, Franz."

Franz frowned. "It was a far different time, and a far different world then."

"That it was, Franz. That it was."

"Much consulting in the Boy Scouts?"

"Franz, no, this is only a consulting job. I'm going to Houston, okay? Nothing else," Dan said, not quite lying. His first flight did indeed go to Houston, although Franz didn't need to know that it was only the first leg of his long journey. "What do you know about Amalgamated Phosphates?"

"I know it is a big international company. They have mines all over the world. They are based in Johannesburg. That's all I know. Is this who you will be doing this consulting for?"

"Yes, that's who I will be working for," Dan said, giving up way too much information, but he needed to know more about the company.

"What do you know about mines, Herr Kruger?"

"Enough that they're paying me handsomely."

"So no more adventures?"

"No, Franz, no adventures. I'm a little too old for that." Dan scowled. He had left his sense of adventure in an unmarked grave of a close friend, in the jungle, a few hundred miles south of here.

"*Och.* Yes. No more adventures for me, except when Hilda tries out a new recipe!" Franz said and they both laughed. Dan finished his cigarette, flicked the butt out the window, and rolled it back up, sitting back to savor the cool air. He looked out the window and watched the countryside go by, thinking about mundane things.

Franz put a tape of German drinking songs in the tape deck and sang along as he drove.

When they arrived at the international departures terminal, Franz parked at the curb and retrieved Dan's suitcase from the trunk. Dan held out his hand and they shook.

"Auf Wiedersehen, Herr Kruger."

"Goodbye, Franz. Thanks for everything. I'll see you in a few months."

"Would you like me to stay with you in case there is any trouble with your flight?"

"That won't be necessary, Franz. You go to one of the strip-clubs here in town and enjoy yourself," Dan said with a sly wink.

"Ha! You are funny! I will leave you now. Have a safe journey," Franz said and got back into the car, driving off with a screech of the tires.

Dan picked up his suitcase and entered the terminal. He stepped up to the Continental check-in counter, thankful there was no line. He was greeted by an attractive black woman with a British accent. He handed over his passport and with a few keystrokes of her computer, she found his reservation.

"Any checked baggage today, Mr. Kruger?"

"One," he said, and placed it in the space for checked baggage. She put a tag on the handle and handed him his itinerary, along with his passport.

"I already have my boarding passes."

"Very well, I have you checked all the way to Kotara, Korotogo. Where is that?" she asked, curious.

"It's near Fiji," he said. "I never heard of it before two days ago myself."

"Pleasure holiday?"

"Business, unfortunately."

"Your flight has already started to board, and it departs from Gate 3 in fifteen minutes. Go to the right and make a left at the end. Have a pleasant flight and we hope you've enjoyed your stay here."

Dan thanked her and walked rapidly in the direction she'd indicated, going through a cursory security checkpoint and passport control manned by a bored local police officer, had his passport stamped, and found the boarding gate as soon as he rounded the corner. He handed over his boarding pass to a uniformed flight attendant. She glanced at it, tore off the stub, and handed it back to him. Dan headed down the jet way and onto the Continental L-1011 wide body, and found his seat. He sat down and looked around, noticing first class was virtually empty, which suited him fine since he wasn't in the mood for any conversation.

After he got himself settled into the plush leather seat next to the window, another flight attendant came up to him, checking his boarding pass again to ensure he was not one of the unwashed masses from coach. When she was satisfied he belonged in first class, she offered him a hot towel, which he declined.

"Anything to drink, sir?"

"I'll have a Jack Daniels and Coke, please," he replied. He sat back and looked out the window, watching the ground crew preparing to move the mobile jet way in preparation for departure. Out of the corner of his eye, he saw the last few stragglers walk hurriedly past him to find their seats in coach. The flight attendant returned with his drink in a glass tumbler and he thanked her. She told him they were preparing to depart, and asked if he could buckle up his seatbelt. He complied and sat back again, sipping on his drink. He liked free booze, but he'd have to watch it or he'd be completely shitfaced by the time he got to Korotonga.

He then thought of the information packets the South Africans gave him to read, and he mentally kicked himself for putting them into his suitcase, which was now sealed in the plane's cargo hold. He mindlessly looked out the window as the aircraft was towed away from the terminal, and he vaguely heard the safety briefing given by the head flight attendant over the intercom.

The aircraft taxied to the end of the runway, and Dan felt and heard the engines throttle to full power. The L-1011 started to move, gaining speed as it went, lifting into the sky in the hot, humid afternoon air. The flight would be a short one, two hours and forty minutes, and he settled into the seat with his drink and an airline magazine he'd found in the pocket in front of him.

He must have drifted off to sleep, because the next thing he knew they were descending into Houston and the flight attendants were busily going through the cabin preparing for landing. The landing was a good one, smooth as silk, and when the plane rolled out, Dan looked out the window again. It was the first time he'd been on US soil in more than ten years, and he wasn't sure if he should be happy or saddened by the fact. As soon as the plane stopped at its assigned gate and the captain turned off the fasten seatbelts sign, he stood, and was the first off the aircraft. He quickly walked down the jet way and followed the signs for Customs. There, he handed over his passport to a stern looking US Border Agent, who gave him a cursory look to compare the passport photo. The agent asked if he had anything to declare, he answered that he didn't, and the agent stamped the passport.

"Welcome home, Mister Kruger," he said, handing Dan back his passport.

"Thank you, it's good to be home," Dan said, not knowing if it *was* good to be home or not. Things had changed so much here since the last time. He walked through and found a monitor that listed all the flights and quickly located his, leaving from the domestic terminal, and it was on time. He'd have a three-hour layover so he took his time walking there. First thing he did was exchange some Belize currency for US dollars at a kiosk. He'd need some cash if he was going to be a few hours. It felt odd hearing English spoken everywhere.

He found an airport bar only a few yards from his flight's scheduled departure gate and sat down on a stool at the far end, where he could watch the travelers. He ordered another Jack and Coke and absentmindedly watched a Houston Astros ball game that was on the TV behind the bar. He thought about phoning his sister in Wilkes-Barre, but he'd not spoken to her in years and decided against it. He sat there, dinking his drink and eating shelled peanuts from a bowl on the bar, ignoring the other travelers until he heard his flight called for boarding.

This flight was another Continental Airlines L1011, and again he sat back quite comfortable in his first class seat for the four-hour flight to Los Angeles, where he had another three-hour layover and did the same thing, except he purchased a few cartons of cigarettes and a half-gallon bottle of Polish vodka at the duty free shop in the international terminal. He sat in the terminal bar, drinking and awaiting his flight, pushing the feeling in the back of his mind that something was wrong with this whole thing further back into the reaches of his thoughts, and daydreamed about a very attractive blonde sitting at the other end of the bar reading a paperback novel.

The TWA direct flight to Nadi, Republic of Fiji, boarded and departed on time, and he quickly settled into the first class seat on the 747. The flight attendant brought him a flute of real French champagne and gave him a dinner menu bound in leather. This was the life. He sat in relative luxury and thought about the other flights he'd had in the past, the cramped, noisy confines of cargo aircraft, and smells of sweat, fear, piss, and vomit permeating throughout the cargo hold, and thanked himself for never having to do that again.

After the aircraft took off and leveled off at cruising altitude, he ordered dinner that was brought to him on real bone china and flatware wrapped in a linen napkin. Again, he smiled, thinking of all the horrible Air Force box lunches he'd forced down his gullet in the past.

If the guys in 5th Group could see me now!

Then a dark cloud crossed his face, remembering that most of his friends from 5th Group were dead now.

He smoked a cigarette after a nice dinner of lobster tail and sirloin steak, then reclined his seat back fully and drifted off to sleep. This flight would be eleven hours and he fully intended to get as much sleep as he could before arriving. Then he remembered he'd have one more flight from Fiji. Strangely, this had no flight time or flight number listed on his itinerary. Only the airline, one he had never heard of, *Air Kotara*. He figured it must be a local puddle-jumper.

He woke with a start to a dimmed cabin, realizing that at some point in his slumber, a flight attendant must have covered him with a blanket. He looked at his wristwatch and saw that he'd been asleep for nine hours. He was stiff all over and his ankles ached, so he stood to get the blood flowing again. He went to the washroom, and after relieving himself, used the toiletry kit that the airline had given all the first class passengers to brush his teeth and shave. After wiping off the excess shaving cream, he splashed some water on his face. He found a flight attendant, requested a cup of coffee, and returned to his seat. A few minutes later, the same flight attendant came back with a china cup and sat it in front of him on his tray. He wondered how anyone could stay that cheerful on a job like that, cramped every day into a metal tube with hundreds of strangers.

She told him they would be landing in Nadi in an hour, and went to attend to the other passengers. Dan sipped his brew and looked out the window at the growing light. The ocean below was still dark, but at 35,000 feet, it was brightening to a new day. He tried to figure out the local time, but the past day and alcohol left him confused and addled, so he decided to check a clock when he got to Fiji.

The flight landed right on time, and because this flight was only half-full, he made it out and through customs in no time at all. Although he'd been told he was checked all the way through to Korotonga, he had to retrieve his baggage from the carousel and carry it to his next flight. He searched around the small terminal, finding no information on Air Kotara, and this left him a little on edge.

There were armed soldiers walking around, and he wasn't sure what would happen if they asked him to open his suitcase and they discovered the pistol. It surely wouldn't be pleasant in this South Pacific paradise; he was sure of that.

After searching, he found a desk by a door that had a sign over it reading 'Air Kotara.' He set his suitcase down, leaned on the desk, and looked around. Seeing no one, he sighed and lit a cigarette. He felt like he'd been hit by a freight train at this point and wanted this to be over with, first class or not.

The door by the desk opened then, and followed by a blast of hot, humid air, a short, reedy white man wearing an old WWII leather flight jacket, and equally old US Army Air Corps peaked cap with a 'Fifty Mission' crush, walked through wiping his hands on an oily rag. He had a smoldering Lucky Strike dangling from his lips and gave Dan a sideways glance.

"Is this where I need to be?" he asked the man.

"I dunno. Is it?"

"I'm supposed to fly to Korotonga today."

"Are you Captain Kruger?"

"Yeah."

"Then you're in the right place. I just finished getting the bird refueled and all the cargo is loaded. Follow me," the man said, heading back out the door. Dan picked up his suitcase and followed the man.

"Are there any other passengers?" he asked.

"Nah. I should have met you at arrivals, but I had a magneto problem in one of the engines."

"Did you say magneto?" Dan asked. He stepped out into the morning sun and stopped dead in his tracks. Sitting on the tarmac not thirty feet from the building was a battered old Douglass C47. Although the olive drab paint was old and faded, he could plainly see that it used to be Army Air Corps.

"Yeah, magneto. I've been having a problem with it for the last week," the pilot said. When he realized Dan wasn't right behind him, he stopped and spun around. "What's wrong?"

"Is that what I think it is?" Dan asked in astonishment.

"Yep, A Douglass C47 Skytrain, or as the Brits called them, Dakotas. Ain't she sweet? I bought it surplus in '46 and have been flying it all over the South Pacific since," the man said, flicking the rest of his cigarette out into the wind with a wide, toothy grin.

"Jesus!" Dan said, and resumed walking towards the plane. He followed the pilot up the folding aluminum steps into the fuselage and was again hit with a heavy fist of heat and humidity.

Although it had been a while since Dan had been in a C47, jump school at Ft. Benning, Georgia, to be exact, he remembered how the stairs folded and the door shut and latched. That chore done, he followed the other man up the aisle towards the cockpit.

"Thanks for getting the door. The stairs get sticky sometimes," the pilot said.

"No problem," Dan replied. As his eyes adjusted to the dark interior, he took in the cargo contents, mostly medium sized cardboard boxes, a cage with a few live chickens, and a few white Styrofoam crates marked **LIVE LOBSTERS-PRODUCT OF MAINE.**

"Someone's eating well," Dan muttered.

"Yeah, the president. He gets in these moods. This month it's Maine lobster. Last month it was Russian caviar."

"There must be a shitload of money in phosphates."

"I wouldn't have a clue, Captain. I just fly. The president is rather generous though. He bought me a C119 Packet when he wanted his new car delivered."

"Mighty nice of him," Dan remarked.

"I thought so. Anyway, there's two seats up front here you can sit in, or since my co-pilot is ill today, you can sit up in the cockpit with me."

Dan tossed his suitcase onto one of the seats behind the cockpit, and followed the pilot, settling into the right hand cockpit seat.

"Oh, I'm forgetting my manners. I'm Joey Sutcliff. I was a captain too, Army Air Corps from '41 to '46."

Dan shook his hand and found the man had a firm grip. Joey showed him where the spare headphones were, where to hook them into, and how to use the intercom. He donned the headset, and sat back while Joey professionally and efficiently went over each step on the printed checklist.

Dan slid the Plexiglas side window open to get a little air, and soon Joey had both Pratt & Whitney radial engines fired up and idling smoothly.

Over the radio, Joey asked, then received permission to taxi out to the end of the paved runway.

As soon as a Qantas 747 cleared the runway ahead of them, permission was granted for takeoff, and the old Dakota leapt down the runway gaining speed. Before he knew it, they were airborne, leveled off and heading northwest.

"I've leveled out at 8,000 feet. I've got no oxygen, so this is as high as I'll take her. The trip will be about three hours," Joey said over the intercom, lighting a Lucky Strike with a match, one handed. Dan took this as a cue to light his own cigarette, and settled in for a long flight.

The open cockpit window let in enough air to cool the inside of the plane, and compared to the sweltering heat of Nadi, it was refreshing.

Joey turned out to be a rather pleasant fellow, albeit a little gruff. Dan found out he was from Cincinnati, Ohio, and had flown transports in Europe out of England until right after D-Day in Normandy, and was transferred to the Pacific.

After the war he'd come home to find his wife had split to parts unknown, so he'd taken what money he'd saved during the war, bought the C47 and settled in Korotonga, flying a thrice-weekly cargo and passenger service between Kotara and Nadi in Fiji. He would, and had, flown to other places in the South Pacific, though that was chartered and cost more than the usual Monday, Wednesday, Friday hop across a few hundred miles of ocean.

Although sparsely accommodated, the flight was a pleasant one, and as the hours zipped by Dan smiled inwardly. He looked out the spotlessly clean Perspex windscreen, and could see the island ahead of them.

Joey deftly swung the Dakota westward, and turned 180 degrees, dropping in altitude as he pointed the nose of his aircraft north of a silty brown river.

"Is that the president's house?" Dan asked, pointing to a large white British Colonial style house that sat high on the hill north of a small village or hamlet at the mouth of the river.

"That? Oh no, that's the major's house," Joey replied with a chuckle.

"Major?"

"Yeah. Retired Brit. Still thinks the *Raj* was the Jewel in the Crown of the Empire. Wot wot!"

"No shit?"

"I shit you not, Cap'n. He and the rest of the British officer class, after leading their army to a glorious defeat in Singapore, spent the rest of the war in Jap prison camps, then decided to come back to his ancestral home here on Korotonga. The Presidential Palace is south of the river, set back into the jungle a bit."

"Bastards gave up," Dan muttered more to himself that to Joey.

"That's right. His family owned most of the sugar cane plantations on the island before the war, so he came back to oversee the operations, and stayed."

"How is the sugar cane business?" Dan asked

Deftly banking the DC3 northward over a vast expanse of empty jungle, Joey replied, "Not as good as it used to be. Right now the one mill left makes about enough to handle the domestic demand, and service a few bootleg distilleries making rum and vodka on the side. Pretty good stuff if you ask me. I'll tell the guy who runs the stills to look you up if you're interested."

"I would be, Joey. So, back to the major, no official capacity?"

"Nothing official. Since the last coup, the Brits and the Americans closed down their consulates so he's kind of a diplomat of sorts. Not that anyone needs one. About seven countries have embassies in Fiji, so if you have a problem and need to go to an embassy, most likely I'll be the one flying you there."

"So he's basically a pompous pain in the ass."

"Pretty much," Joey said, made some slight corrections with the flight controls, and lowered the landing gear. Ahead of them, over the flat black painted nose, Dan could see the white expanse of the runway. He also noticed that there had been no radio contact between Joey and the airport, and they came into the place as if they owned it.

Dan was astonished to see that the airstrip was still of the crushed coral and Marston mat from the war, and commented to Joey about it as the taxied up to the front of a whitewashed concrete building with a rotating red and white beacon on its roof. No control tower or radar could be seen anywhere.

"All we need. Nothing bigger than my C119 ever lands here, so once in a while we roll out some fresh coral on the thing. It's been holding up nicely," Joey replied, shutting down the engines.

"Thanks for the flight, Captain." Dan climbed out of the cramped copilot's seat.

"It's Joey, and no worries. Anything at all you need, you come ask for me," Joey told Dan, taking his hand in a firm grip.

"Wilco, Joey." Dan nodded and exited the cockpit. He grabbed his battered suitcase and headed down the narrow aisle towards the rear cargo door. When Joey opened it, hopped down, and lowered folding aluminum stairs, the pair spied a battered old Land Rover, followed by two World War II vintage Canadian military pattern trucks.

The trucks sidled right up to the Dakota and without being told what to do, some dark-skinned islanders in sarongs began to unload the aircraft. Dan turned to look where Joey had gone, but he had vanished.

"Captain Kruger?" a voice right behind him called out, and a viselike grip of a massive hand fell onto his shoulder, spinning him around like a toy.

"Yeah, that's me," Dan said, looking at the mountain of a man that faced him. Towering over Dan's 6'2" frame by at least five inches and outweighing him by one hundred pounds, the man's sheer bulk was impressive. What stood out to Dan, however, besides the sheer bulk, was the rapidly graying close cropped red hair, and a perfectly waxed handlebar mustache, topped off with a maroon beret with the British 1st Airborne Division flash. He was also dressed from head to toe in the obsolete British Tropical Green uniform, shorts, and hobnail boots.

The man snapped to attention and saluted in the British fashion, palm facing outward, and reported firmly in a Scottish accent thicker than six-day-old haggis, "Sir! Sergeant Major Neville MacDevitt, at your service!"

"At ease, Sar' Major. I'm not in uniform, so we'll eschew the military protocol."

"Fine by me, sir," MacDevitt said, taking Dan's suitcase, and unceremoniously tossing it into the back of the Rover. The two men climbed into the cab, and MacDevitt behind the wheel. He put the still-running vehicle into first gear, and sped away from the terminal in a cloud of white coral dust.

"No customs stamp?" Dan asked.

MacDevitt turned right onto a raggedly maintained road that had once been a two-lane asphalt highway cut through the jungle and ran along the beach.

"Nae. Not many people come and go anymore, so the president doesn't think it necessary to keep up with it."

As far as the US government is concerned, I'm still on Fiji...

Dan didn't say another word after that, and MacDevitt wasn't forthcoming with any more information. He sat back and looked at the scenery passing by. It could be anyplace tropical in the world, it was so generic. Beautiful, but generic.

Scattered around through the coconut palms were grass shacks of various states of repair, some unattended fruit and vegetable stands along the road, and...

Where is everyone?

In any other place like this in the world, he'd expect to see a fair number of people coming and going, milling around outside their huts, children playing. There was no one.

It was starting to creep him out, then he remembered it was Friday, and the kids should be in school. They rounded a curve, and sitting on a log was an ancient woman in a flowery, brightly colored muumuu. While the garment may have been cheery, her whole demeanor was cold and heartless.

Her black eyes locked onto Dan's and wouldn't let go. In spite of Dan's broad smile and friendly wave, the woman's face remained stony. After they passed and the woman was rapidly disappearing in the rearview mirror, Dan could still feel her icy stare boring holes into the back of his head.

Once they came closer to town, Dan did see more people, though not what he expected. MacDevitt again made small talk, pointing out the fruit and vegetable grocer, doctor's surgery, post office, police station, and school, where he did see a large gaggle of children playing rugby.

"Before we cross the Kota River and onto the Presidential Palace, to the right we have the Grand Hotel. It's become our unofficial second headquarters, Captain. A fine drop and a good meal can be had for a song, and the place is clean and tidy. It also has the best view on the whole bloody island."

"I'll definitely have to check the place out, Sar' Major."

They sped across a wooden bridge that spanned the Kota River and crossed over some narrow-gauge railroad tracks that MacDevitt pointed out were the main conveyance from the mine to the pier. There was a gas station and auto repair center on the corner of the main road and a side road that wound its way uphill, only to be swallowed by the jungle eastward.

Travelling about two hundred yards farther, they came upon a huge wall of bougainvillea to the left, blocking all view to anything beyond. To the right was a clear, wide strip of pure white sand that led to the ocean farther west. MacDevitt slowed the Land Rover and made a left, turning into a cut in the hedge, and Dan was greeted by the sight of two islanders, obviously Army because of their dress and equipment. Again, 1942-era Tropical Greens, British army helmets, MkIII SMLE .303 rifles, and could that be an actual tracked Bren Gun carrier behind the tiny red and white striped guardhouse?

"Shit. Please tell me again what year this is?"

With a little wink, MacDevitt said, "Aye, I found it a bit queer at first meself. It's what the Brits left the government when they gained their independence, and I find it quaint."

"Quaint it is, Sar' Major. Is it practical?"

"Who's gonna be invading us, Cap'n? Certainly not the Japs again."

"You do have a point."

"The only other group that could be of any danger the president had disarmed during the last coup."

"The people?" Dan asked

"The police."

The guards dressed in their finest WWII uniforms came to attention when they saw the Land Rover approach, and opened the gate smartly, saluting until the vehicle was well past them.

Instead of taking the main driveway that curved to the right and up to the front of the palace, MacDevitt turned to the left, onto a dirt track that led off northward on the compound to a two-story wooden barracks, shaded by tall coconut palms.

MacDevitt grabbed Dan's suitcase and bounded up the stairs smartly, as if every step was a parade. Dan followed, looking around briefly to get his bearings.

On the top of the stairs was a long, narrow walkway that led the length of the entire building, a door every ten feet, with a light outside, doormat, and a number painted on the door itself.

Pulling a huge brass fob out of his pocket, MacDevitt located the key and opened a door, ushering Dan inside. He was hit right away by a cool blast of air from an ancient Coldspot air conditioner mounted in the rear wall. There was a chest of drawers, a large wardrobe, refrigerator, toaster, electric kettle, and an old Philco cabinet radio in one corner. A second door led to a shower and toilet, and as a nice after touch, a sliding glass door in the rear led to a modest, and private veranda.

"Here's your quarters, sir," MacDevitt said, handing Dan the key. "The president is up at the mine today with half our detail and won't return until sometime Monday afternoon. He makes the trip every fortnight, and is usually gone over the weekend. Take this time to get oriented, rested, and over your jetlag. I'll come around for you tomorrow morning, say, 0730 to get you sorted with some uniforms."

"Sounds good to me, Sar' Major," Dan said tiredly.

"The president is a good bloke, although a tad squirrelly. He does insist on the uniforms, yet in deference to our multi-national makeup, has allowed our men to wear the headgear of our previous national units."

"Hence your Red Devils beret."

"Exactly, sir. Now I'll leave you to it," MacDevitt said, coming to attention, making a perfect about face, and marching out of the room, shutting the door firmly behind him.

Dan looked around once again, sighed, and had enough energy left after thirty hours of travel to strip down to his underwear and fall on the bed. As soon as his eyes were closed, he was snoring away peacefully.

CHAPTER 3

The first meeting Dan had with the president was terse and to the point, and left him a little stunned.

MacDevitt had provided him with uniforms, and with a green beret placed perfectly on his head, he'd marched into the president's office when bade by an assistant, came to attention, and saluted. "Sir, it's an hon—"

"Your record is exceptional, Captain. I'm sure I will be pleased with your work," the leader cut him off, and without so much as a by your leave, stood and walked out of the office through a side door.

Dan stood there gob smacked for a moment, letting his eyes scan over the president's sparsely appointed desk as a matter of habit, memorizing a few notations written in sloppy penmanship on a battered blotter. This moment alone was fleeting, as another door opened to the left, and a short dwarf of a man entered. Dan immediately thought his first job must have been sitting under a bridge passing out riddles.

"I am Tiki. I am the president's personal assistant and secretary. From now on, anything you wish to convey to His Excellency, you will go through me," the troll-like man said in clipped English. He handed Dan a slip of paper. "This is the president's schedule for the next fortnight. It is not for public dissemination. Work your staff's rosters around it. He will be protected by no less than six of your men at one time while outside of this compound."

Dan looked down at the bi-weekly schedule and saw that it was completely blank of any notations at all. "Understood."

"Good. Also, I'm sure the sergeant major has already told you of the two main ground rules you must abide by, which I will repeat. Number one, the palace interior is off-limits to you and your men unless otherwise bade by His Excellency or myself. The exception is the palace kitchen and servants' dining hall, where you're expected to dine."

"Yes, he's told—"

"Number two—and there will be no exceptions to this rule—you violate this rule your contract will be voided, is that understood?"

What a smarmy little fuck, Dan thought. "Yes sir, I understand completely."

"Absolutely no travel outside of Kotara alone. It is for safety reasons we must put this restriction on you. Your predecessor was murdered by marauders in the jungle north of town a few months ago, so it is imperative to follow these orders if you wish to stay healthy."

"Marauders?"

"Yes. Hoodlums. Loyalist pigs who wish to bring back the old president's regime. I assure you that will not happen, for I saw the old president swing from a rope," the elfin man spat angrily, fire in his eyes. "The army has them cornered in the jungles in the north, and we will soon be done with them for good. Good day, Captain."

With a flick of a wrist, Dan was dismissed. Although for a few fleeting moments, he was infuriated, that washed to the rear of his mind. He left the presidential office and found his way back to his quarters.

That meeting was several months prior, and Dan had rapidly folded into the tedious routine of making it look like he was actually doing something every day. The president never stepped outside the palace compound, except for the biweekly excursion to the phosphate mine.

While there were no TV stations, the island did have one government controlled radio station, and the president would pontificate to the people every Friday evening from a remote transmitter in his office.

Dan had thought, not for the first time, that the president himself was making his job all the easier. Dan and his men hardly had to do anything except foot patrols overnight in the palace compound and the convoy to the mine and back.

Easy money...

"Huh?" Dan said, startled.

"I said *easy money*," MacDevitt repeated, handing Dan an ice-cold bottle of Miller High Life, sitting down across from him at the table on the rear veranda of the Grand Hotel.

"If it was any easier, we wouldn't even need to get out of bed."

"Aye. It would've been nice if my time in Africa had been this staid," MacDevitt agreed. He'd spent a number of years as a true mercenary, fighting bush wars all over the Dark Continent with a true legend of the business, Mike Hoar, and Dan never tired of the sergeant major's colorful stories.

It was Friday afternoon, and it was Lieutenant Nguyen's turn to command what Dan now called 'The Dog & Pony Show'; the president's biweekly trip to the mine, leaving half the men at Kotara with nothing to do except drink lots of alcohol. Dan and MacDevitt were sitting at what was now considered 'their' table. Even the few locals that came into the place didn't sit there.

MacDevitt had been correct those many months ago when he picked up Dan at the airport. The Grand Hotel did indeed have the best view on the island, save for the major's house high on the hill, although Dan had yet to go up there himself.

Although he'd been meaning to go up and play nice with the British major, his heart wasn't in it. For the time being he'd be playing at avoiding the major at all costs.

His thoughts went back to what MacDevitt had said. While it was indeed easy money, more money that Dan had ever had the pleasure to make in his life, there were things that were not sitting right in his mind, things that were starting to bother him. He'd not brought these issues up before tonight, and he was thinking one more beer and he might open up to MacDevitt, whom he was as close as he'd ever been in the military to what would be called a buddy.

Dan leaned back, kicked his feet up onto the railing, and took a long pull of his beer. He looked westward towards the rapidly setting sun, and then to a ship that, with the help of an ancient coal burning tugboat, was chugging out of the channel through the reef.

Off to the west, another similar ship was waiting to come into port. And so it seemed to never end.

"Neville, how long have you been on this island?" Dan asked.

"Three years, Dan," the Scotsman answered.

"And in these three years, have you ever noticed anything odd about the place?"

"Fuck, laddie, it's all as queer as a three-pound note."

Dan lit a Marlboro with his Zippo lighter, took another pull from his beer, and pointed at the ore ship leaving port. "Like that ship, Sar' Major. Do you notice anything odd about that ship?"

"A boat's a boat, Dan. They're all the same to me."

"Nev, look at it. That mine up there we go to, the one where, because we're not *native*, we can't step on sacred grounds so we have to wait outside when the president goes for his tours, is supposedly cranking out fucktons of phosphate, enough to pay us what we're getting paid."

"Okay, laddie. I'm following you, I think."

"If they're pumping out so much phosphate, why is that ore ship that left sitting as high in the water as it did when it came in yesterday?"

"Bloody hell. I never took notice before you pointed it out."

"A ship that's loaded with any cargo would have its gunwales awash when it left port."

"I'm getting what you're saying now."

"Since we're not allowed inside the fenced off area of the mine, we don't know, to be honest. Does it *look* busy to you?"

"Nae, and all the mining equipment outside looks old and rusted."

"The only thing that looks busy around there is the little narrow-gauge railroad. That's busier than dogs with two dicks, but you never get to see the phosphate ore."

"Because they're tarped-over to keep the dust down."

"So they tell us. And again, the trains. How convenient it is that there's a slight northward cant to the pier, so that if two ships are on the docks, you can't see what the train is doing, unlading or lading anything?"

"And the train never goes on the dock without there being two ships in port." MacDevitt grinned broadly.

"Exactly."

"You know, laddie, this pisses me off. The bloody bastards got me to let me guard down, get complacent about me area."

"Don't let it get to you. I guess I'm naturally paranoid. Here's another thing," Dan said, leaning forward and lowering his voice. "All the people. Where the fuck is everybody?"

MacDevitt didn't say a word, and Dan could tell he'd hit a chord.

"I mean, shit, Nev. When I was in Vietnam, we'd mosey into a hamlet, and the first thing that would hit us was that all the men were gone. There'd be kids and old people. That's when we knew that Charlie had them. This is supposed to be some South Pacific island paradise. There's no war going on here, except for those 'marauders' I was told about when I first got here. I haven't heard one shot, not one goddamn gunshot since I got here, save our own firing at the range."

"Aye, saw the same thing in Africa. There's nothing, there's no war going on here."

"So what have we got? We've got a few cops here and there to give us dirty looks, kids, and old people. No younger, or military age people, very few 18 to, say, 40 years old. And that, my friend, stinks rotten to the highest heaven. There's supposed to be close to fifty thousand people on all of the islands combined. It's like the whole goddamn population of Hinesville, Georgia vanished overnight."

"What the bloody hell are they hiding?"

"I don't know, and I'm not digging being bullshitted like this," Dan hissed, stubbing out his cigarette angrily.

"I suggest caution, laddie."

"Yeah, so do I. It's my turn to buy the next round. I'll be right back," Dan said, standing and grabbing the empty beer bottles.

"That being the case, I'll have four fingers of Cutty Sark, neat, in a rocks glass."

Dan disappeared into the hotel leaving MacDevitt alone on the veranda. MacDevitt stared out at the rapidly departing ore ship, and watched the dance of the tugboat and the new ship coming into port with a growing dread.

He'd known right away that Dan was different, smarter than the rest before him. He was hoping he wasn't *that* smart. Apparently he was wrong.

"Neville, laddie," he whispered to himself, "methinks you are going to be right in the middle of a right wee mess sooner that you thought..."

⧽⧽⧽⧽⧼⧼⧼

Dan slid up to the bar and waved Flo over. Flo was a Polynesian beauty, and she and her French-Tahitian husband owned the Grand Hotel. He was the only other Caucasian on the island, kept to himself for the most part, and was even aloof to Maxime Chauvet, a former lieutenant with the French Foreign Legion and a member of Dan's protection detail.

Maxime, despite being French, was an okay guy and pretty good soldier. He was in the hotel that night too, and was with his unlikely best friend, Sergeant Ernst Bauer, ex West German GSG-9. They were sitting across the bar from where Dan was standing, waiting to order his round of drinks.

Both younger soldiers were well on their way to a drunken stupor, though they still behaved well.

"*Capitaine!*" Maxime shouted out to Dan across the bar. "Please help me! Explain to my Bosch *ami* that Flo does not love him the way he loves her!"

Dan looked over at the always stern, now saddened Teutonic face of Ernst and shook his head. "Ernst, give it up. How long have you been trying to get into her pants? She's not going to leave her husband for the likes of you, that's for sure."

Flo came up to Dan and her smile sent shivers down his spine.

Gotta admit, ol' Ernst, she does do a number on a guy simply by smiling at him. While Ernst sobbed into his pint of lager, Flo glanced over to him, shrugged and said to Dan, "Sometimes he gets so *untidy*, *non*?

"Untidy is a good word for it, Flo," Dan agreed, and ordered a beer and four fingers of Cutty for MacDevitt.

He picked up his drinks, and called out to Maxime across the bar, "Look after him tonight."

"As always, *Capitaine!*"

Dan made his way back to the table on the back veranda and sat down with a plop and a release of air.

"Sometimes the world does that to ye, aye?" MacDevitt said, taking his drink and sipping slowly, deep in thought. He reached into his trouser pocket and produced an ancient, battered meerschaum pipe, filled the bowl with fresh tobacco, tamping it with his thumb.

With great showmanship, he produced a single wooden match, struck it on the heel of his boot, and with flourish, lit the bowl in five or six quick puffs that surrounded his head in a blue cloud of sweet-smelling smoke.

"So now what?" Dan said quietly. The sun had dropped below the horizon, and now red, green and blue party lights came on to light the deck gaily. Some of the rare locals began filling up the bar, spilling out onto the veranda, and somewhere someone dropped some coins into an old, 1940s vintage Rock-Ola jukebox that thankfully had some newer 45s loaded into it.

A teenage island couple giggled and danced close to one another to the sounds of Jerry Rafferty, and Dan looked away.

"Aye. The question of the hour, laddie. Now what?"

"I think you and I should keep our eyes open and see what we can come up with."

"Aye, and keep it between us?"

"Yes. No one else, as yet. Right now there's only one other on our team that I trust implicitly, and that's Lieutenant San. Nguyen. He and I go way back, 1968 in fact, to my first A-Team in Vietnam. He was once a tough ARVN sonofabitch," Dan told MacDevitt, pronouncing the acronym ARVN, or Army, Republic of Vietnam, as *Arvin.*

"I see. You two never let on that you were close."

"He's a stoic bastard. Besides, he doesn't have a whole lot left to be happy about. He told me all his family got stuck when Saigon fell, and he's been floating around ever since, a man without a country."

"I think we're all a little like that."

"He told me in confidence, only after I pried a little too hard. He's a very private man."

"I will remember that and respect it in the future. That's settled. Shall we forget all of this dark, seedy rot for a wee bit and sit here, watch the young people have a bit of fun, and let's get drunk, shall we?"

"Let's." Dan smiled and held up his bottle. "Cheers!"

MacDevitt did the same. His easy smile hid well the troubled thoughts going through his mind, and for a time it was another drunken Friday evening at the Grand Hotel.

➤➤➤◄◄◄

Dan awoke with a start in the darkness, and he looked around, trying to discern where he was. As he gained his wits, familiar sounds rushed in to remind him that even though it was pitch black in his room back at the compound, he was safe and sound.

In the darkness he stumbled over to the refrigerator, opened it, and using the interior light, looked at his wristwatch. It read ten minutes past three in the morning. Dan grabbed a two-liter bottle of whole milk and skulled it in a couple of gulps.

Placing the now empty bottle on the kitchenette countertop, he shut the fridge door and stumbled back into bed. When he heard the compressor kick in on the fridge, he again sat up, a serious look painted across his face.

He went to the wardrobe and pulled out a few articles of clothing. A black t-shirt, black sweatpants, and a pair of black Converse All-Stars. Donning the clothes quickly and silently, he moved over to the sliding glass door that he'd thankfully oiled. It slid open without a sound.

He almost floated across his private veranda, and stood breathless at the rail. He had a two-meter drop down to the soft grass below, but beyond the coconut palms that provided shade in the afternoons, there would be no cover at all for fifty meters to the bougainvillea hedgerow that surrounded the palace compound.

Although the moon had set more than an hour ago, there were so many stars he could make out certain landmarks without difficulty. As he was going to vault over the railing to the yard below, he thought he heard something and stopped dead.

Not moving a muscle, he scanned the area. Coming from around the east side of the barracks, two figures crept along the grass between the hedgerow and the building.

One figure stopped, and the other followed suit.

"What is it?" one whispered.

Dan made the voice to be Archie Davies, one of his men, an ex-Royal Marine.

"I thought I heard something," said the second man, and with the Georgia twang, it could only be Cletus Snodgrass. A Vietnam vet like Dan, he'd served with the 173 Airborne Brigade.

Both held onto their Sterling submachine guns a tad bit tighter, neither sacrificing trigger discipline and, as one of Dan's old platoon sergeants used to say, they kept their goddamn booger hooks off the bangswitch.

Good job, guys.

Dan decided he might be able to use this to his advantage when trying to sneak back in. If caught, he'd say he was testing the perimeter defenses.

He waited on the veranda until they moved off, and slid slowly off towards the west, and the front of the compound. When he was certain they were out of earshot, he vaulted sideways over the railing in one swift movement, gracefully landing soundlessly onto his feet on the courtyard below.

Taking one last look around, he sprinted directly at the hedgerow, not stopping until he was flush with the side. Going slowly, he inched backwards into the thick bush, willing his body to melt into it.

To Dan's surprise, it wasn't as thick as he'd first imagined, and it appeared to be hollow inside, like a long, green tent. Dan had never seen anything like it before, and decided to use it to his advantage for now. Depending on what he and

MacDevitt found out would determine whether he'd report it or not say a word about this huge lapse in security.

It was like a long, green tunnel with a soft, damp floor. Absolutely no sunlight could penetrate the outer layer of green, so nothing grew underneath. It was a superhighway, and Dan made record time making the length of the hedge, and was soon behind the guardhouse by the compound's front gate.

He could hear right away the two Korotongan soldiers talking, though he couldn't make out their words. He could smell their cigarettes also, and he knew they were wide awake, but no telling how alert they were.

He backed away into the bush, creeping silently through the other side of the row, and found himself on the outside of the compound, about one hundred meters north of the guardhouse. He crouched and looked around to get his bearings, and not seeing another soul around, chanced a sprint for about another three hundred meters northwest, across the empty road, across a wide beach, and right up to the harbormaster's shed.

He sat down, back against the wall of the shed, to catch his breath. He could plainly see the sterns of both ore ships tied alongside the pier. Both were registered in Panama, and that was fairly typical.

That was yet another thing he'd bring up with MacDevitt. None of the crew was off the ship, even though they stayed for the better part of 72 hours. He'd never seen, not once, a sailor from one of the ships in town, or at the Grand Hotel. He was sure Flo and company would love to see the money some sailors would spend on booze alone.

He stood, reaching for the doorknob. He'd forgotten his lock pick set in his haste, and was rewarded by the doorknob turning freely. He opened the door and entered the dark space, shutting the door behind him. Noting that the blinds were drawn, he chanced turning on the desk lamp in front of him.

A halo of yellow light illuminated a circle on the cluttered desk. He sat down on a rickety chair, quickly reading everything he could see. Things began to fall into place, and he soon got a rough idea of what was going on.

Sort of.

Lots of invoices, all from Amalgamated Phosphates, Johannesburg.

No surprise there.

He dug deeper into the pile and started to look at what the invoices were for. Mainly chemicals. Acetic anhydride? Chloroform, sodium carbonate, ethyl alcohol? The list went on and on. Large quantities of these chemicals too. He knew that in some mining operations, copper, silver, and gold especially, that there were a few chemicals one would use to extract the payload from the ore, acids mostly. Wasn't phosphate just lying there? You only had to dig it out of the ground like coal. Cheap to get at, invaluable, and worth its weight for fertilizers all over the world.

He spied a green ledger book and opened it, flipping through the pages. While he had no idea what he was looking at, or what exactly he was looking for, little things began to pop out at him.

This ledger had to do with what was only labeled as 'Product,' dates this product was shipped, in metric tons, and on what ship. No other hint at what the product was. What did resonate with Dan, and he'd mentioned it to Neville earlier, was that he thought the ships were going out as empty as they'd come into port.

Yet not quite, he found out.

Several hundred metric tons of this "product" were going to these ships on a weekly basis, just not the several hundred thousand tons of phosphates that *should* have been going out on them. That was a problem in Dan's eyes.

He was baffled. His head was beginning to hurt, and all the beer he'd drank last night at the hotel was starting to catch up to him. He jumped at a sound he thought he heard from outside, and quickly glanced at his watch.

Five AM. The sun would be up soon. He switched off the light. When he reached the door, he opened it carefully, sticking his head out into the growing light. With a sharp pain to the back of his head, followed by a flash of light in his eyes, darkness engulfed him.

CHAPTER 4

The sharp pain had now faded to a dull ache, and again Dan found himself disoriented.

He slowly and painfully raised himself to a sitting position, clearing the cobwebs out of his head. His vision refocused, and he discovered he was sitting in a locked jail cell.

On the other side of the ancient iron bars was a battered old wooden desk that was heaped with various papers. Dan heard movement, and sat still.

A tall, thin, dark skinned man wearing a blue police uniform appeared, carrying a white porcelain mug. He glanced into Dan's cell and noticed he was awake.

"I see you're back with the living, Captain."

"I'm lucky you didn't kill me. What did you hit me with?"

"Hit you? Neither I nor any of my men hit you, Captain. You were found unconscious on the wharf, and I was summoned," the police officer said. "Would you like a cup of tea?"

"Yes, please," Dan said, and began searching his pockets.

The police officer disappeared and Dan could hear the rattling around with a pot and cups. He returned with another steaming cup and sat it on his desk "The door to the cell isn't locked, Captain. I only put you there because of the cot."

Dan stood and exited the cell, and sat in the chair in front of the desk, facing the officer.

"I believe these are what you were looking for?" the police officer said, sliding over Dan's lighter, cigarettes, and a thin wallet with his ID and some cash.

"Yes, thank you," Dan said, taking a sip of the hot tea.

"Forgive me for my rudeness. I am Revu Karalaini, chief of police. I am sorry to have not introduced myself sooner."

"I'm sure that president would be most grateful for that. He seems to not like you or your men all that much."

"I am well aware of that situation, Captain. What about you? How do you feel about us?"

"I was raised to respect the police, to trust them. They were the good guys."

"True. Unfortunately, sometimes in politics, things get a bit blurred. Tell, me, what were you doing on the docks so early in the morning?"

"I was out for a morning jog."

"A morning jog?"

"Yes, that's about it."

"You weren't doing recon, maybe for a little sabotage?"

"Sabotage? What in the world for?" Dan laughed. "That, sir, is the last thing on my mind. Why would I bite the hand that feeds me? The president pays me quite well to protect him. I, for one, intend to continue to get paid."

"Isn't that what you American Green Berets are good at? You're all one-man armies, if my memory serves me correctly."

"No, sir, we're trained as what's known as 'force multipliers.' Sure, back in the very early years, before we were an actual unit, we were part of the OSS—Office of Strategic Services— and did all kinds of nasty tricks to the Germans in Europe and the Japanese out here in the Pacific."

"Yes, I know of the OSS. Our fair president claims to have served with them, fighting a clandestine war against the Japanese during the war, however, I am not the only one who will tell you he was merely a collaborator. He collaborated with the Japanese to not only make his life comfortable, but to ensure his power after the war."

"That doesn't surprise me," Dan said.

"How does a force multiplier work?"

"Actually, it's kind of boring. Not at all like what Hollywood would like you to think."

"Humor me, Captain," Karalaini said in a tone that told Dan that, while he wasn't a prisoner, he still wasn't quite free to go quite yet.

"The way it was originally thought up, was to have twelve men, an 'A' Team, all highly trained in their respective military specialties. Medics, explosives experts, small arms men, communications experts, linguists. We all had to speak the host or enemy country's language fluently, that sort of thing. All were to be airborne qualified, all the men were to be at least a sergeant or higher in rank. Professional soldiers."

"It sounds very intriguing."

"It is," Dan agreed. "It's what drew me to them in the first place. You had to be a volunteer, and only a handful would get in."

"Their missions?"

"The main mission of a Special Forces A Team is to, like I said, be a Force Multiplier. Parachute clandestinely behind the Iron Curtain into Eastern Europe, make contact with resistance fighters, and train them in guerilla warfare tactics."

"So these twelve men, could make a—"

"Company of soldiers, and that company could train up a battalion, and so forth."

"A very unique concept indeed."

"It worked rather well for us in Vietnam. We trained whole villages of Montagnards, mountain tribesmen, and they fought the Viet Cong quite bravely and valiantly."

"Did you enjoy doing that, Captain?"

"Chief, no one really likes war. Did I enjoy my role in freeing oppressed peoples? Yes, I enjoyed in immensely."

"Is that what that means on your lighter?" the chief asked, pointing at Dan's Zippo.

"Yes, it's the Special Forces motto, in Latin. *De Oppresso Libre*. To free the oppressed."

The police chief leaned back in his chair, staring at the ceiling with a faraway look in his eyes for some time. Finally, he snapped out of whatever trance he was in and dropped his gaze to Dan once again. "You're free to go, Captain. I may wish to speak with you in greater depth later."

Dan smiled and stood. "Thank you, sir. You know where to find me if you want to talk again."

"Yes I do, hopefully not passed out on the pier in the early morning hours."

Dan exited the police station. After being inside the darkened concrete building, he was momentarily blinded by the bright morning sun, and squinted to see his wristwatch. It was past 9AM. He walked to the Grand Hotel, where he was met by a smiling Flo, who went automatically to the beer cooler. She had the door open and her hand on a bottle of Miller High Life before Dan could get her attention.

"No, Flo, I think I'll have a coffee this morning, and maybe breakfast."

Flo vanished into the kitchen, returning with a mug of coffee on a tray, along with a bowl of sugar and tiny pitcher of milk. Dan thanked her and asked if he could use her phone.

After she placed a battered old Bakelite rotary phone on the bar top and was out of earshot, Dan dialed the number from memory. After a few rings, a static-filled connection was made.

"Security, Corporal Jimenez speaking. How may I help you?"

"Jimenez, this is Kruger. Could you get the sar' major for me please?"

"Sure thing, Cap'n. He's right here, going over next week's duty roster."

There was the sound of some rustling, then MacDevitt's voice came on the line. "Sergeant Major MacDevitt speaking, how may I be of assistance?"

"Nev, it's Dan. How would you like to have breakfast with me this morning over at the Grand?"

"I've already eaten in the mess, but I guess I could come over for a Bloody Mary."

"I'll see you in fifteen minutes," Dan said and hung up the phone. He called out to Flo again, ordered breakfast of scrambled eggs, toast, bacon, and a Bloody Mary for MacDevitt, and retired out to the table on the veranda.

>>><<<

MacDevitt showed up the same time Flo did with his breakfast. Disregarding ceremony, Dan dug into the hearty meal. He'd not realized how hungry he was until the hot meal was in front of him. He said nothing until he was finished, and poured a fresh cup of coffee from the carafe Flo had brought out.

"Cap'n, if you don't mind me sayin', you look like something the cat dragged in."

"I feel like it," Dan said. After checking that there was no one within earshot, he related everything he did after MacDevitt left him off at the barracks the night before. When he was finished, MacDevitt let out a long, low whistle.

"What do you think this 'product' is?" he asked.

"Beats me. I'll wager my left nut it isn't phosphate."

"Aye, I agree. And the police chief. That was an odd event."

"True. It was like he was fishing for something, some trigger word I'd say to allow him to let on to what his real motives were."

"I can tell you this much. He hates the president. Taito Yasi is the police chief's half-brother. Or should I say, *was* his half-brother."

"That's news. He didn't lead on. He was adamant that Ilikimi was a Japanese collaborator during the war."

"Doesn't surprise me. He's been doing nothing but lining his own pockets since I've been here. Whatever money the government is getting for the mine, it sure isn't going to the government's coffers."

Dan raised his eyebrows. "What gives you that impression, Nev?"

"Oh, nothing specific," MacDevitt backpedaled. "Look around at the infrastructure."

"Yeah, it is falling apart."

"There's been talk for years now of getting new turbines for the hydroelectric dam up north. We even had a few guys from Siemens out last year, but nothing else has ever been said about it."

"And the lack of decent phone lines."

"Or roads, or anything."

"Yeah, the money has to be going somewhere," Dan agreed. "And that somewhere is the president's pockets."

"Is that our business, Dan?"

"If the money is coming from where I think it's coming from, yes, I do think it's our business."

"If that's the case, then what?"

"I'll figure that out once I have enough intelligence. The first thing I'm going to do is find out what's going on at that fucking mine. Once I do, we'll go from there."

"Alright, laddie. It's your funeral. I'm with ya' with whatever ye might find out."

"Tell me about it, Nev."

"I'm with ya, Dan. What about the others? Some of them might not take too kindly to havin' their teat lopped off mid-suck."

"I agree. We'll have to tell them about it, get everyone's input. Everyone has to be in full agreement. If not, I'll leave it lie right there."

"Full agreement?"

"Yes. No sense going into this with less than that. If we don't have full cooperation on this, who's to say they might not tip our hands to Tiki or Ilikimi? We'll call a meeting in my quarters, say at around 1900 tonight."

"Done. I'll spread the word," the gruff Scott said.

"Good, now let's get out of here and make it look like we're being productive."

Later that evening, at exactly 1900, half of his unit not with the president up at the mine site was standing in front of Dan.

He looked each in the eye, and only saw raw curiosity. These were professionals. Most, if not all had some combat experience and would spot a line of bullshit a mile away. He'd give it to them straight.

He took in a deep breath, let it out, and began to speak. It took him more than twenty minutes, and to his surprise, he wasn't interrupted once. To a man, they all kept their peace until Dan was finished speaking.

He finished up with, "Guys, I know some of you are thinking right now that this is none of our business. Who gives a fuck what the president does? He's not *our* president. Well, I know, and I hear you. I also hear you about the money. We're making damn good money here, and for all intents and purposes, we're also on the road to becoming filthy rich, so why not let the guy make his money, and we make ours? It's not like Ilikimi is asking us to do anything illegal, is he?"

When he concluded, everyone was left alone in their own silent thoughts. Dan let everything he'd said sink in for a few minutes and cleared his throat to speak again.

"Guys, I'm not asking for a decision tonight. I still need to talk to the other half of the team. It's Saturday night. Those of you who don't have watch, go out to the Grand Hotel and have a good time. The sar' major and I will speak to the others on Monday, and I'll want your decision by Wednesday. Before then, nothing has changed. Do your job in a professional manner."

There was some milling around, and one by one, they all filed out of Dan's quarters. Even MacDevitt didn't stick around like he might on some occasions, leaving Dan to his own thoughts.

He flipped on the ancient radio, and as the vacuum tubes warmed up and began to glow, he picked up an AM station from Honolulu and smiled. While it wasn't the best reception, it was playing songs from his childhood that made him happy. He had a strong feeling that it would be a long time before he was happy again.

He'd sat at his tiny desk and not for the first time, tried to write a letter to Maria. Like every other time, he thought he sounded too sappy and moronic, so he crumpled the sheets of paper up and tossed them into the wastepaper basket at his side. His heart ached for her, and he didn't know how to let her know that he was still thinking of her.

He was standing to head to the refrigerator when there was a rapping on his door. He opened it slightly, cautiously, to find three familiar faces staring at him from the outside walkway, and opened his door wide.

"I didn't expect any of you back so soon," he said, ushering them back into his room. He turned off the radio and sat down at the desk.

"Sir, I hope you don't mind us coming back so soon," Booker Davis spoke. His African features didn't reveal his feelings, but his eyes were soft and caring. Like Dan, all three who came back were American, and veterans of the recent war in Vietnam. Booker had served with the 173rd Airborne Brigade.

"Not at all. What's on your mind?"

"Sir, it's like this," José Jimenez, ex United States Marine Corps, said, "when we came home from the Nam' we felt, well, empty."

"Yeah, empty, sir," Cletus Snodgrass, US Army 25th Infantry Division, agreed.

"We felt like victory was ripped from us," Jimenez continued. "We all did a good job there. , You should know as well as all of us, we got robbed, spit on, and then forgotten."

"I'm in one hundred percent agreement with you," Dan said quietly. "I felt the same way."

"We had a chance to do some real good in the Nam sir, and they took that away from us."

"Sir, what we're trying to say is we, the three of us, see the same fucked up shit you did. The ships leaving no lower in the water than when they arrived, the people, or the lack of people. Weird shit going on up at that mine. Something fucked up is going on around here, and I don't dig it at all," Booker Davis stated.

"Sir, back in '68 I got into some trouble with the law," Jimenez said sheepishly. "The judge gave me the choice of going to jail for two years or joining the Marine Corps. I joined the Marines, and they sent me to Vietnam. It made a man out of me, and I'm not running around with a bunch of cholos in South Phoenix."

"You're a hell of a Marine, José," Dan said.

"Sir, I've got a son. He's back in the Barrio. He wants to be a Marine like me one day. He also wants to learn to fix airplanes, so I send all the money I make here back home so Juan never has to make the choices I made, or the stupid ones. He wants to be a Marine because he's proud of me. Honestly, I have never done anything for him to be proud of. If by sticking with you we can do some good, maybe we can leave a little better world for our kids, you know?"

"So sir," Cletus spoke up, "you find out what this fuck Ilikimi is doing and we'll fuck up his world."

"Thanks. This means the world to me. And you hit the nail on the head earlier, Jimenez. I too felt empty when I left

Vietnam, like something was stripped from me. With all of your help, we all can get that feeling back."

"Hooah!" Booker shouted.

"It's getting late. I'm sure some of you are on the overnight shift tonight. We'll speak of this again Wednesday," Dan said with a wide grin and ushered them out of his room. After he took a hot shower he drifted off to a peaceful sleep serenaded by the air conditioner rattling away in the wall.

The next five days dragged on, and after each step of the way in what Dan had planned, things got a little dicier. Monday's chat with the rest of the men went about the same as the first talk, and same as before, he gave the men until Wednesday evening to make up their minds. By that evening, things were so tense he felt like screaming.

When MacDevitt knocked on his door around 2100 Wednesday evening, Dan was wound up like a 13-day clock. When he was told the news, that all of the men were behind him one hundred percent, it was like a huge pressure valve was released, and yet, simultaneously, a huge weight was placed on his shoulders.

They sat up until late that night, going over maps and making plans, until they had a decent working plan before them. MacDevitt didn't like it, and he voiced his opinion. Dan wouldn't have any of it. The plan would go on as it stood.

They met in front of the barracks early the next morning, Thursday, loaded up the Land Rover, and headed out of the compound. When they reached the front palace gates, the Korotongan soldier on duty asked where they were heading off to so early in the morning.

"Aye, the Cap'n here and I have a wee wager on who's the better shot with a pistol, so we're heading out to the range to settle it."

"I wish you both good luck!" the soldier said, and waved them past.

MacDevitt was driving, and he made the right hand turn onto the main road and sped off for a few hundred yards, and then again made a right hand turn onto the jungle road that led through the thick vegetation and to the mine, ten miles away.

They drove on silently, the triple-canopy swallowing them up, bright daylight turning to a dark twilight as they ventured deeper and deeper into the island's interior. Dan checked his map one last time and signaled for MacDevitt to pull over.

"Are ye sure ye wantin' to be going about it this way, Dan?"

"Yes, it's the only way. Do exactly what I said to do when you get back to the compound, and all suspicion will be deflected away from you and the rest of the men."

"What about you?"

"I'll be fine. You make sure that parcel I gave you winds up where I told you to put it, or else I'm fucked. I won't be able to do anything more, okay?"

"It'll be there, Cap'n," MacDevitt said, firing up his pipe and puffed away as Dan changed from the tropical green British uniform over to his old OG 107 slant-pocket jungle utility uniform and jungle boots.

He then took some web gear out, with two full one-quart canteens, first aid pouch, compass, spare magazine pouches for the curved 30-round magazines for the Sterling sub machine gun, which he loaded, but didn't cock.

His final act was to take some dark face paint and darken up all of his facial features, ensuring all his pale skin was covered. Looking in the side view mirror of the Land Rover, he nodded to himself in approval and placed an olive green patrol cap on his head.

"Again, I wish you'd reconsider, but I'm afraid that point is moot," MacDevitt said sadly.

"It is. It's the only way. Give me about an hour, and get back to the compound. It's about an hour on foot from here. I'll need about an hour to scrounge around. Remember that when you get back. I'd rather the alarm be raised after I've already been through instead of them waiting for me when I get there."

"Yes sir," MacDevitt said somberly.

Without another word Dan slid silently into the jungle and vanished like he'd never been there. It happened so fast that MacDevitt had to blink a few times.

Dan took to the jungle like he was born to it, and rapidly made progress, stopping and checking the map and compass every fifteen minutes, correcting his route accordingly.

He soon came upon the two foot gauge railway line that ran directly into the mine itself, and followed the tracks on a parallel path a few feet into the jungle until he hit an old overgrown chain link fence blocking his way. This he followed back towards the rail line, and simply walked through the fence at the open gates, disappearing again into what looked like sugar cane that had gone wild.

Deeper and deeper he progressed into the mine area, until he got close enough to where he began to hear the sounds of people and voices. A woman's high-pitched wail broke the stillness, and Dan dropped down to a prone position, silently low-crawling towards the cries.

He was on the top of a low hill, at the very edge of the overgrown cane, and parted some leaves to get a clearer look.

He fervently wished he'd not seen what he saw. Right away he saw the source of the wailing, a Korotongan woman, crying and pleading, was being held back by soldiers, while another soldier, this one an NCO, had a young, skinny Korotongan boy kneeling down in front of a huge pit, an old Webley .445 pistol cocked and held to the boy's head.

When Dan realized what was in this pit, he nearly vomited. Covered with quicklime to accelerate decomposition and mask the smell, the huge pit was stacked with the dead bodies of countless Korotongans.

Keeping his cool the best he could, he watched as the sergeant pulled the trigger on the pistol, heard the muffled 'pop' and saw the body flop limply into the pit. The woman shrieked and lunged at the sergeant. The soldiers simply pushed her aside and marched off, leaving her to sob uncontrollably in the dust next to the pit.

Was it her husband? Her brother? Son? Dan couldn't know. Whoever it was, what was done was barbaric. He pulled out a pair of binoculars and scanned past the horrid pit and the woman, further into the mine area.

A vast overhead covering of camouflage netting had been strung up over what looked like acres and acres, and there was a huge production line manned by hundreds of Korotongans, being closely guarded by armed soldiers.

This must be where they made the 'product,'

Looking further out and to the right he saw a train being loaded by hand. Each tiny rail car was being loaded piece by piece with large white bricks, and when each car was fully loaded, a dark tarpaulin was tied to the top of the car, hiding what was inside.

Dan backed away into the cane until he was well hidden, and sat up. He scratched the back of his neck and thought for a few minutes.

Now he knew where most of the people went. He also knew it wasn't phosphates that was making all the money. What was the product? Cocaine? Nah, not coke. The Columbians had that little morsel all tied up. Hashish or heroin, that's what it had to be.

He followed the train until he found the last loaded car, and checked to see if anyone was close by. Seeing no one, he pulled out his Camilus fighting knife and sprinted to the side of the rail car, cutting the rope holding the tarp, and in one motion, reached in, pulled out one of the 'bricks,' and ran back into the cane field.

Taking his knife, he poked a hole in the side of the soft, plastic brick and tasted a tiny bit of the white powder inside. He spat it out immediately, his thoughts confirmed.

Heroin.

A shitload of it. He'd never seen anything of this scale before in his life. They must be cranking out tons of the shit weekly. It had to be making the president *billions* of dollars.

Dan was seething. Those two fucks who first offered him the job fucking knew what was going on, and how he felt about it. They had to have known, and lied to him to get him to take the job. They were going to pay dearly for that mistake.

Dan left the brick on the cane field and moved away from the mine, back along the railroad tracks, through the gate, and back into the jungle. He stopped for a moment, swallowed some water from his canteen, then headed off westward.

His mind was going a mile a minute, and it took him a moment to register what he was seeing. A sarong clad, bare-chested islander holding a rifle was barring his way, not ten feet in front of him.

As soon as that one appeared, three more materialized from the jungle and Dan stopped dead in his tracks. He had begun to raise his hands in surrender when the first one took what Dan could now see was an ancient Japanese Arisaka rifle, and in a flash, swung the butt forward, catching Dan on the cheek, knocking him out cold on the floor of the jungle.

CHAPTER 5

Dan awoke in complete, utter darkness. His head pounded where the Korotongan had got him good with the rifle butt. He pushed that pain to the back of his mind and tried to figure out what had happened to him.

He smelled the dark, loamy odor of damp soil, and wherever he was, it was cool to the point of being chilly, and he involuntarily shivered for a moment.

A yellow flicker of light caught his eye off to the left, then it grew closer. He could now see from the shadows cast by the light he was in some sort of completely enclosed room.

The light grew closer, and along with it, a woman's pleasant voice singing an island song. In spite of the circumstances, Dan thought it was quite beautiful.

He sat up on the old metal cot he'd been placed on, and looked over to see an old, battered Dietz kerosene lantern held out at arm's length enter the room, the arm attached to a plump Korotongan woman with a round, pleasant face.

When she saw that Dan was awake, she smiled broadly, set the lantern down on a bedside table, and sat on a stool close to the bed.

Calling out over her shoulder, again in Korotongan, she produced a bowl of water from under the table along with a cloth and began tending to Dan's wounds.

"Do you speak English?" Dan asked.

"Yes, I do. Not very good. My husband will be here soon to talk to you."

"Who's your husband?"

"That'd be me, laddie," a familiar voice rang out from the darkness, and the large frame of MacDevitt squeezed through the narrow door.

"Neville? What the fuck is going on?" Dan shouted.

Taking another chair, MacDevitt sat down next to the woman. "Shut yer' geggie. No one here is gonna be hurtin' ye. It'll take a few minutes to explain, so if ye would, let me talk for a bit."

The big bear of a man took the woman's hand gently, looked into her eyes, smiled, and turned back to Dan. "Dan, allow me to introduce me wife, Lara. You've already met her brother, Revu Karalaini."

"The chief of police?"

"Aye."

"How come you never told me this before?"

"Because we weren't sure we could trust you completely. I apologize. We should have told you sooner."

"I understand operational security. But please ask your guys to stop clocking me in the head, okay?"

"Aye, Cap'n," MacDevitt said, shooing the woman out of the room.

"So where is this place?" Dan asked.

"It's about three hundred feet under the mountain. The Japanese dug miles of the things during the war, and never got to use them, which is all well and good, because now we control them. Like I said, they dug miles of them. We've only been able to map out what we recon to be about twenty percent."

"Who's 'we', Nev?"

"You'll see in a minute. Again, I'm sorry for keeping you in the dark for all this time, it's just that we weren't completely sure we could trust you with our plans."

"What are those plans?"

"To take back the Republic, Captain," an unfamiliar voice spoke out from the darkness. A slight balding man emerged, and MacDevitt stood up, almost bashing his head on the low stone ceiling, producing a stool for the man.

After sitting down, the man took Dan's hand in a surprisingly firm handshake. "Captain, I am Taito Yasi."

"I thought you were supposed to have been hanged?"

"That was the illusion, Captain. A loyal patron volunteered to take my place that day, a widower with no children. He'd fought by my side against the Japanese, and wanted to see me free in order to take back the country at some point."

"And no one could tell who was behind the hangman's hood, eh?"

"That is correct, Captain."

Dan wanted to ask them how they pulled off that little coup, but didn't want to get distracted from the current story. "So where do I fit in into all of this?"

"Neville and Revu have told me great things about you, Captain Kruger. How your Special Forces work, your role in this great military unit, and how this might help us take back our island from that psychopath, Nete Ilikimi."

"In theory, myself, Neville, and the rest of the men could indeed train up a fighting force. However, there are a lot of variables."

"Like what, Captain?"

"Like timeframes. How long you'd want to willingly wait for the men to be ready. It doesn't happen overnight. It takes months to train up a force the size we may need."

"What else?"

"Well, there's the who. Who would we train?"

"My police force," Revu Karalaini said, walking into the now crowded room.

"Are you sure they'd be one hundred percent loyal?" Dan asked.

"Without a doubt."

"How many of them?"

"About four hundred."

"And Nete's army?"

"It's about three thousand strong, Dan," MacDevitt said.

Dan let out a long, low whistle, looked at the three faces in front of him, and shook his head. Wheels were spinning deep in his gray matter. Nothing was said for well over five minutes, until Taito asked, "Captain, will you or won't you help us?"

"Mr. President, I'm not digging the odds. Give me and the sar' major here a few days to come up with a game plan, and I'll let you know if it's viable or not."

"Very well," Taito said pleasantly. "Did you find anything out about what is going on at the mine site? We had never been able to get close enough to discover what they were doing there, only that they were doing something nefarious, and taking a lot of our people for slave labor to do it."

"That's what I thought you'd ask me first. To be honest, after I saw enough, I scooted out of there pretty fast. What I did see was heroin production on an industrial scale, and slave labor that would make every Nazi very happy indeed."

"That was what I was afraid of, Captain. I was told ten years ago that mine was about dried up for any more phosphates."

"So now what?" Dan asked.

"You have complete freedom here, walk around and get your bearings. I'll send someone to get you something to eat and drink, and I'll let you two work something out."

"Thank you," Dan said, and the two Korotongans vanished into the darkness.

Dan faced MacDevitt and sighed. "Another fine mess you've gotten me into."

MacDevitt laughed and picked up the lantern. "Let's get out of here and get some fresh air."

"Sounds good to me," Dan said, following the big man through a maze of passageways that Dan could tell by the slope of the floor were leading them both further up to the surface.

When they reached the surface and walked a few feet, Dan looked back and could barely make out the tunnel's entrance. It was that well hidden into the landscape. The two men walked a bit further until they found some shade, and sat down with their backs against a few fallen logs.

"So the dead president isn't dead, and wants me, and you, to build him an army to overthrow the president I'm being paid to protect," Dan stated, pulling out a pack of Marlboros and lit one with his Zippo.

"I think we can do it."

"Four hundred against three thousand. Last time I checked those weren't great odds. And the cops were disarmed. Where do you suppose we get the weapons?"

"That's not a real problem. Hirohito left all the weapons we'd ever need here in 1945," MacDevitt stated proudly.

"No shit?"

"I'll show them to you in a bit. First, Nete's army is mostly paper tigers. They're tough with old people and kids, but I doubt seriously they'll put up any kind of stiff or lasting resistance."

"That's yet to be seen."

"And they're spread out over the entire island," MacDevitt said, crouching down with a twig and drawing a rough sketch in the dirt of the main island. "Look here. Besides the main barracks at the palace in Kotara, there are three more. One on the very northern tip, one on the southern tip, and one on the east side of the island, not including the men posted at the mine."

"Alright, I'm following you now."

"Since I've been involved in a few underhanded coups in my time, know that the only ones we care about are the soldiers at the palace. Once we overwhelm them, then we occupy the palace compound, there's only one other thing we'd need to take control of."

"Two things. The radio station and the mine."

"I stand corrected. The radio station *and* the mine."

"Alright, we'll need good recon on the mine site, manpower, schedules, everything we can learn. If we can't take it over, maybe we can isolate it from the rest of the island somehow, make it irrelevant."

"Agreed. The same goes for the other three barracks. We cut them off, make it impossible for them to come to the aid of whatever mayhem we plan to unleash on the palace," MacDevitt stated flatly, standing and kicking dirt over the drawn map with his booted foot. "Now what?"

"Now, Sar' Major, you take me to see this vast array of Japanese Imperial Army weapons you've got stashed away."

"I haven't seen it all, mind you. I'll take you there now," MacDevitt replied. He marched over to the tunnel entrance, followed by Dan.

For nearly an hour the pair traveled through the maze of tunnels, and the further they got, the more impressed Dan was. There were full barracks, latrines, baths, a hospital, kitchens and mess areas, all held in stasis, circa 1945.

The one thing that kept nagging Dan on this tour wasn't the tunnels themselves, it was the dampness. Everything was moist, and dampness was a modern weapon's nemesis. While he hoped it wouldn't have affected this stored stockpile, it had been more than forty years and he didn't count much for miracles.

Finally, they reached the end of a long tunnel. The way was blocked by a thick wooden door, heavy steel chain, and ancient padlock. MacDevitt produced a key, opened the lock, and pushed open the door.

Taking the lantern from MacDevitt, Dan cautiously entered quite a large room compared to all the others. In the cone of yellow light emitted by the lantern, the pair could see stacks and stacks of old, water stained wooden crates of various sizes.

They were all marked in Japanese, so neither knew what was inside each box.

"I guess it's like Christmas," Dan said. "We'll have to find out what's in them by opening them up."

MacDevitt vanished for a few moments and came back with another lantern and a crowbar that had been left by the door. He handed the crowbar to Dan, who walked over to a stack of long crates and attacked the lid.

The old wood splintered easily, Dan peered into the crate, and his shoulders fell. MacDevitt, who'd been lighting the second lantern, came up behind him and looked over his shoulder.

"So, laddie. What do you think?"

"I think we're fucked." Dan picked out a rifle at random to get a better look at it. There looked to be ten rifles in each case. He tried to open the bolt and found it was completely rusted closed, in spite of the heavy slathering of Cosmoline grease. "Yeah, we're fucked. Even the wood stocks are rotten."

"All of them?"

"Yeah, I don't even need to open the rest of the crates. This one was on top, and water trickles down. Look at the bottom crates," Dan pointed out, and they both could see they were black with rot.

"Bloody hell!"

"Yeah. If they'd been stored in a dry place, they would have lasted a few hundred years. The moisture ate through them. They were, by the look of them, early war Type 99 Arisakas. 7.7mm. Late war stuff was junk. These were still made with precision and would have probably served us well."

Though all of the cases were marked in Japanese, some had Arabic numerals on them, and Dan knew right away the '7.7mm' was the Arisaka rifle's ammunition. He went over to the stacks of cases of ammunition. "This is our last chance. If the ammo is fucked, there's no reason to even try to restore some of the rifles."

The crowbar came up, and again, the old, rotted wood splintered easily. Dan reached in and pulled out a cardboard box that disintegrated in his hand, leaving two 5-round stripper clips of 7.7mm ammunition that had seen better days. The once shiny brass and copper now had a thick growth of green crud growing on them and Dan threw them in disgust into the darkness.

"Let's get out of here."

"Aye, and get some fresh air."

MacDevitt led them back out to a clearing in the jungle. The two men sat down on the damp ground and looked at each other for a time.

MacDevitt was the first to break the silence. "Now what?"

"While I'm not entirely sure, the last time I checked, you couldn't have a coup and overthrow a despot with no guns."

"Aye, makes for a lopsided gunfight, matey."

"Nev, I'm going to assume that you didn't follow my orders and report me rogue?"

MacDevitt's face split into a huge grin. "Nae. You're worth more to me alive that ye would be swingin' from a tree."

"I'm going to take off for a bit, and I'm probably going to have to leave the island for a few weeks."

"It'll be status quo here until you say otherwise."

"You'll have to tell Taito and Revu. You can reassure them that I may still be able to pull this one off. Though I'm not altogether sure on the how part yet, they don't need to know that. When we get back to the compound, I'll go and see that little fucking worm Tiki and let him know I've got a family emergency back in the States I need to attend to."

They headed back through the jungle to where MacDevitt had hidden the Land Rover. Changing back into his uniform, Dan took a washcloth and water from his canteen and removed the fading green face paint from his face.

When they were back on the road westward towards Kotara, Dan asked, "Do you know Joey Sutcliffe? Is he trustworthy?"

"That I don't know. I do know he keeps to himself."

"I think we're going to need him in order to pull this off."

"Aye. I'll suss him out."

"I'll poke and prod him too. I'm going to try to get a hop to Nadi with him tomorrow on his usual flight." A kernel of an idea for a plan was formulating in Dan's mind.

"You know what, Dan?" MacDevitt said. "It feels good to be back in the saddle so to speak. Doing some good for once."

"I agree, Nev. Oh, and one more thing, if you can get it to me before I leave. The Army. I'd like to have a rough estimate on their TO&E," Dan said, sounding out each letter, *Tee Oh and E.* Each military had a TO&E, or Table of Organization and Equipment, spelling out everything that unit took with it, from main battle tanks down to how many sheets of toilet paper each man was allotted.

"I'm on it. I'll have that to you before afternoon tea."

"That soon?"

"Aye. It's set up in the British model, of course, and the fools actually gave me a printed copy when I first got here in '83."

"That solves that problem."

"Aye. I'll also let the men know what's going on. I'm sure they're eager to finally do something."

"Yeah, temper it with a little restraint though. It's still going to take months to get all of Revu's men trained, even if I can get the weapons, *and* get them into the country sight-unseen."

The pair got back to the compound at 3PM sharp, and MacDevitt dropped Dan off at his quarters to shower and change. This Dan did, and when he was dressed, marched himself over to the palace to speak with Tiki. After waiting an hour in an anteroom, Dan was allowed in to see the president's secretary.

"What is it I can do for you today, Captain Kruger? It is getting quite late."

"I'm deeply sorry for troubling you with this, but I've received a letter from my sister back in Pennsylvania. It seems my father is quite ill and might not make it until the end of the month. I'm going to need to take a few weeks off to fly home."

"Oh, that is terrible news!" Tiki gasped. "Of course. Take a few weeks and spend them with your family."

"Thank you, sir. I've put Lieutenant Nguyen San in charge, and the sar' major as second until I return. Now, if you'll excuse me, sir, I'd like to go and pack."

"By all means, Captain, and we'll look forward to your return."

Not if you knew what was running through my mind right now, you little fuck...

Dan smiled politely and went back to his quarters.

The next morning, he was up before the sun, and was met by MacDevitt at the foot of the stairs. Taking Dan's suitcase, he tossed it into the back of the Land Rover and hopped in behind the wheel.

"Nev, how come you never let me drive?"

"Because you Yanks will never understand how to drive on the correct side of the road."

"Fair enough," Dan said.

"So what did you tell the troll?"

"I told him my father was gravely ill and wouldn't last the month."

"Is that wise, sir? Ye don't wanna go 'round jinxing your kin like that."

"It's okay, Nev. He's been dead for about twenty years now."

"Then that's a good cover story, Cap'n."

"If they decide to dig, I'll be found out. The two Saffers who recruited me knew a shitload of things about me that nobody should have had access to."

"We'll keep our fingers and toes crossed then, shall we?"

Dan closed his eyes and let the breeze caress his face.

MacDevitt pulled the Land Rover onto the grounds of the airport, and drove around the terminal building, across the taxiway, and towards a large corrugated tin hangar that edged up to the jungle and parked next to a side door.

The men alighted from the Land Rover. Dan opened the door and entered the hangar, calling out to Joey, and the sight before him stopped him in his tracks.

"I'm right here!" Joey yelled, appearing from under the cowling of a plane Dan had only seen in old newsreels about the Pacific War. "Oh, hey, Cap'n! I was expecting you."

"You were?" Dan asked.

"Yeah, Tiki phoned me last night, let me know that you would be needing a flight to Nadi ASAP. Family emergency or something."

"Yeah. I need to get to Fiji today, and I wasn't sure what time you'd be leaving."

"I'm usually gone by now, but I was waiting around for you, and decided to work on my little project here," Joey said, running a hand lovingly across the fuselage of the rare bird.

"Is that what I'm thinking it is?"

"If you're thinking it's a Mitsubishi A6M Zero, you'd be correct."

"Shit! Does it fly?" MacDevitt asked incredulously.

"First time was last week. It's been a long time coming."

"Where'd you get it?" Dan asked.

"Out the back. There are about thirty of the bastards that were bulldozed into the jungle at the end of the war. This here is a Frankenstein. It's taken me about twenty years to get enough bits and pieces off of those thirty planes to make one flyable unit."

"I'm impressed."

"So am I," MacDevitt parroted.

"Everything works on it."

"Even the guns?" Dan asked.

"Yep, even the guns. I found a few hundred rounds for the 20mm and the 7.7mm. I had to dig through a shitload of rotten, moldy stuff to make a full combat load. Not that I'll ever want to strafe something, you know, it's fun to have."

"I am impressed," Dan said again, and looked over at MacDevitt with raised eyebrows. MacDevitt gave him back a barely perceptive wink and a nod.

"I guess you're not here to talk about the Zero. You've got a plane to catch," Joey said, beckoning them towards the Dakota sitting in front of the hangar.

While Dan and Joey were climbing into the C47, MacDevitt called out.

"Yes, Neville?" Joey answered.

"I almost forgot. I need to talk to you later. When you get back, would you mind calling in to the Grand Hotel for tea?"

Joey looked at his watch. "It'll have to be a late one, say, around 2100? I've got to go over to Suva after we land in Nadi, and that usually takes a few hours."

"Alright then, a late tea it is," MacDevitt said. He reached out a big, beefy hand towards Dan, who took it firmly.

"Nev, I'll see you in a few weeks. I should have everything sorted by then."

"Take care," MacDevitt said.

CHAPTER 6

Thankfully, the flight was uneventful in the old C47, and Joey, being the excellent pilot he was, landed them right on time at Nadi International Airport.

The pair of expatriate Americans made their way past throngs of Aussie tourists, past the hire car and cab stands out to the main road and waited on the shoulder of the road at a bus stop.

"Now what?" Dan asked.

"We wait for a carrier. It'll only cost us a few bucks Fijian to get to Suva. It's about 120 miles."

Soon after, a decrepit looking Toyota Hilux pickup truck approached and stopped. The rear bed had bench seats along both sides so the passengers would face each other, and a makeshift canvas cover that reminded Dan of the old deuce and a halves they had in the Army.

Joey did the talking to the driver, handed some faded notes over, and soon they were ensconced in the rear, careening down the highway in the direction of Suva.

"How come the trip to Suva, Captain? I thought you had to get back to the States. The only international flights leave from Nadi."

"I've got some unfinished business at the Embassy. It'll take a few days before I can leave for home," Dan lied.

"I get you. I had some shit to deal with like that a few years ago. Goddamn IRS will be the death of all of us, I tell ya." Despite Dan trying his best to get some sleep, the Hilux's springs, combined with the Third World status of the main road, wouldn't allow it. Three painfully long hours later, the traffic grew heavier as they neared Suva.

The main road skirted the harbor, and Dan looked out at some of the same type ore carriers, cargo ships, oilers, and container ships moored there. Off to one side, he spied something else he didn't expect to see.

"Hey, Joey, check it out. A World War II LST."

Joey glanced over and smiled. "Oh, yeah. I know the guy who owns it."

"No kidding?"

"We're not best friends or anything, but yeah, we know each other. We've done business in the past."

"That's pretty cool. Most of them were scrapped after the war, so you don't see a whole lot of them around."

"No, you don't. It's a shame. I heard stories about the Boeing and North American factories. They were still cranking out B-17s, B-24s, P 51s, and as soon as they'd roll out finished, there was a shredder there cutting them up for scrap."

"It's sad to lose all that history." The carrier made its way into gridlock traffic. Horns were blaring and people were shouting. Dan had had enough, and asked Joey what direction the Holiday Inn was located.

"It's south, right along Victoria Parade. Follow this road south and look for the signs to the Museum of Fiji. You can't miss it."

"Okay, I'm hoofing it from here," Dan said, and climbed out of the back of the cramped Hilux.

Joey reached into his pocket and thrust something into Dan's hand. "Here's my card with my telephone number on it. I've got one of the few phones on Korotonga. Give me a ring when you're coming back and I'll make arrangements to pick you up."

"Thanks, Joey. You take care." Dan headed south, sweat pooling down his back. After about twenty minutes of walking, he spied the Holiday Inn sign a few blocks away.

Walking through the front doors of the hotel, he was slapped with a blast of ice-cold air. Thankfully, the air conditioning was working. He walked across the lobby towards the front desk and a smiling Fijian man.

"*Bula vanaka.* How can I help you today, sir?" the man said cheerfully.

"I was hoping to find a room. My other reservations fell through, and I'm kinda' room-less right now."

"You're in luck, sir. We have a few rooms for you to choose from. I have a queen sized mini-suite with a harbor view balcony available. I can give it to you for the price of a single if you plan on two nights or more."

"Two nights is all I'll need, thanks."

"Wonderful! Smoking or non?"

"Smoking," Dan said, and handed over his passport.

The receptionist opened it up, and began to type into his computer keyboard. "American, huh? We don't get many Americans here. Mostly Aussies and Kiwis. Are you here for business or pleasure?"

"Business, unfortunately," Dan said tiredly and handed over an American Express card in his name.

"What kind of business are you in?" the man asked. Dan was irritated. He knew the man was only being friendly and inquisitive, not nosey.

"Import/export."

"Here's your keys, Mr. Kruger, and also your passport and Amex card. The lifts are right over there. It's room 1017. The hotel bar and restaurant open at 4PM. Enjoy your stay!"

At the elevators, Dan hit the 'up' button, and immediately the doors slid open. He looked at the panel in the car, and remembered this was set up in the European style, where the first floor was actually the second floor, and the first floor was the ground floor.

He'd keep that in mind later if he spent a little too much time in the hotel bar. Getting out of the car on the tenth floor, he followed the room numbers around until he found his, inserted the key, and turned to knob.

He entered and tossed his suitcase onto the bed, shucked his sport coat, and headed over to the mini-bar. Finding a beer inside he'd never had before, assuming it was a local brew, he popped the top and took a swig of Fiji Bitter. He was pleased with the taste.

He opened the curtains to the balcony, enjoying the view. He wistfully wished Maria was with him. Chugging the beer, he checked his watch. It was 3:30PM, so he finished the beer, stubbed out his smoke, and stripped for a long shower.

After the shower, still wrapped in a soft hotel towel, he sat down on the bed and opened the drawer of the end table. Finding the local phonebook, he scrolled directly to the yellow pages and quickly found what he was looking for.

He picked up the telephone receiver and dialed the number.

It rang on the other end, then a woman's calm, cool voice in a nondescript American accent answered, "Good afternoon, Johnson's Hardware. How can I help you?"

"Hi there. I was wondering if you had about five gallons of polyurethane paint in royal blue."

"Please hold while I check the stock. It won't be a moment." The line clicked to Musak before Dan had a chance to reply. He was secretly wishing he was a fly on the wall at the other end, and giggled a little, because using the Johnson's Hardware number must have people going batshit crazy at the embassy. The line clicked again.

"Sir? Are you still there?"

"Yes, yes I'm here."

"Would that be for pickup in the store or delivery?"

Will you be coming to the embassy, or do you need someone to meet you?

"I would much prefer delivery, if you don't mind," Dan replied. *No, I need an outside meet...*

"Very well, sir, could I have the address?"

"Number 1 Victoria Parade, downtown Suva."

"Okay, sir, it'll be about an hour, is that alright?"

"That would be fine. And the name is Kruger."

"Alright, Mr. Kruger, our delivery driver should be there within the hour."

There was a click and then dead air. Dan laughed aloud as he placed the receiver back on its cradle.

He'd always been tempted to call the CIA's field agent emergency number to see what would happen. He was about to find out. He knew for certain they weren't expecting that line to ring anytime soon, especially in this part of the world, and he was thinking the entire intelligence section was probably going apeshit right about now, trying to find someone to go out and make the 'delivery.'

He went back into the bathroom, brushed his teeth and shaved, and pulled out a fresh shirt. He got dressed, eschewing a tie, grabbed his Browning 9mm and placed it under his belt in the small of his back, grabbed a fresh pack of Marlboros and his lighter, along with his room key, and headed down the long corridor towards the elevators.

He rode the lift alone all the way to the ground floor, and when the door opened he went straight for the front desk. He told the polite concierge his name, what room he was staying in, that he would be expecting someone soon, and requested the visitor be directed to the outside bar.

The bar had only been open for fifteen minutes, and already it had a few patrons. Dan had to wait for the bartender to finish making a British woman a cosmopolitan before he could get a drink, so he took the opportunity to look around.

Nothing hinkie so far.

When the bartender asked what he wanted, he decided to go all out and ordered four fingers of Jack Daniels over ice. He took his drink out to the open-air lounge and found himself a table with his back to the bay and a view of all the entrances. Dan took a sip of his drink and settled in. He didn't have to wait long. His eyes locked onto the man as soon as he came outside the building onto the patio. A nondescript white guy, five foot ten, overgrown civilian style haircut, cheap, off the rack Sears & Roebuck's suit and tie, and cheap black loafers.

Yeah, he's an Agency drone alright.

When the man looked at Dan for a little too long, Dan smiled, held up his drink, and motioned with his arm to take a seat. When he did this, the guy looked like he was going to jump out of his skin, but quickly regained his composure and headed to Dan's table. When the guy sat down, Dan motioned for a waiter.

"Relax, man," Dan said. "You look like you're about to have a goddamn stroke."

The waiter came to the table. "Could we have two menus, please? And what will you have to drink, mister...?"

"Poindexter," the guest replied. "I'll have a glass of water, thank you."

"Very well, sirs," the waiter said and vanished.

"Dude, seriously. Chill the fuck out. Your face is as red as a dick on a dog," Dan said.

The waiter came back with a carafe of iced water and a glass, and Dan motioned for another four fingers of Jack. The waiter nodded and vanished again.

"What's the emergency, Mr. Kruger? That name isn't on our list..." the man said, stopping himself before he said too much.

"You're a newbie, aren't you? You shouldn't have let that out. But hey, everyone's got to learn some time."

"What is the emergency?" Poindexter hissed.

"Okay, alright. If you would just calm the fuck down and cool your tits for a minute, I'll tell you."

Poindexter took in a few deep breaths, poured himself a tall glass of water from the carafe, and took a healthy swallow. He set the glass down and produced a handkerchief that he blotted his forehead with.

When he looked as relaxed as he'd ever be, Dan started. "About eight months ago, I took a private security job for a South African mining company, Amalgamated Phosphates. Actually, not so much a security job, it was more or less dignitary protect—"

"Wait a minute," Poindexter cut in, "you mean to tell me you're not even Agency?"

"I'll get to that part in a minute, and I'll give you my bonafides to pass on to the station chief before you go so there will be no doubt in anyone's mind I'm who I say I am. Now if you interrupt me one more time, Poindexter..." Dan looked at him for a moment, and when the man said nothing, he continued. "As I was saying..."

For ninety minutes, and four more Jack Daniels over ice, Dan told his story. Poindexter ordered two Fiji Bitters after a while. Dan lit a Marlboro, clicked shut his Zippo, and blew out a stream of smoke rings to lend final credence to his story.

"Holy shit. That's one truly disturbing story."

"No shit, Poindexter. That's why I came to you guys. No, I'm no longer Agency. Still, I find this kind of shit vitally important. The question is, what do you plan on doing with the information?"

"I'm...well, I'm not sure."

"I know. You're a drone, a worker-bee. You'll run what I've told you past the section chief, he'll send a cable to Langley overnight, and you and I will wait for that answer."

"Pretty much."

"I'm booked in here for two nights, tonight and tomorrow. If I don't hear from you by Friday morning, I'll assume that nothing has changed in the Agency and I was correct in my decision to take an early retirement."

"Fair enough, Mr. Kruger. I'll be in touch."

"Is there a number where I can reach you directly?" Dan asked.

Poindexter handed Dan a business card. Dan looked at it and was duly impressed. "Naval Attaché, Lieutenant Commander Hiram Poindexter, it was nice meeting you."

"Same to you, Mr. Kruger. We'll be talking soon."

"I'm sure of it," Dan said and watched the man walk off. He called the waiter over, ordered the surf and turf and a garden salad, and ate in the growing twilight.

Later that evening, he was channel surfing on the big color TV and sipping on yet another Jack when he realized he needed a little cash. He dialed his Cayman Islands bank and requested a wire transfer, in US currency, to his name at the Holiday Inn, Suva. Five thousand dollars would be sufficient, he told the nice lady on the other end of the phone. After he hung up, he hoped that the local Westpac or Commonwealth banks, both Australian, would have enough US currency on hand to cover it.

Sitting there on the bed, phone receiver still in hand, Dan got a wild hair up his ass, and decided to try something.

Remembering the day he met the president, in that brief moment, reading upside-down and memorizing two series of letters and numbers, along with an international toll-free number hastily jotted down on the edge of the president's blotter, he dialed.

After a few rings, an automated voice came on the line, and in German, French, and English asked for an account number. After a few clicks, the voice asked for the passcode number, and Dan dutifully entered the second six-digit number.

He waited yet again for a few beeps and clicks, and the same automated voice provided a menu of options, balance inquiry, transfer, payment, debit, balance. Dan selected 'balance' and waited for a response.

When the robotic, automated voice on the other end of the phone spoke out *eleven digits,* a decimal point, then two more digits, Dan had to hit *'repeat'* several times to make sure he wasn't too drunk to comprehend how much money that was, and double checked that it was indeed US dollars. He ended the call, set the receiver down, went to his suitcase, and took out a pen and notepad.

He then wrote it down, just to see the numbers in front of his eyes.

$17,897,614,357.39

"And thirty-nine fucking cents!" he shouted. Eighteen *BILLION* fucking dollars. He tried to imagine that kind of money, and couldn't.

His mind racing, he picked up the phone again, dialed the Swiss bank account number, and selected 'transfer' this time. He transferred one million into his own Cayman Islands account, hung up, waited a few minutes and checked the balance on his account, discovering that he was one million dollars richer than he'd had a few minutes ago.

He went to the wet bar, poured himself a healthy shot of Jack and went out onto the balcony. He gazed out over the harbor, lit up by the anchorage lights on a plethora of ships.

"Thirty-nine goddamn cents! As if you'd worry about the cents when dealing with that amount of money. President Nete Ilikimi, I do believe you will be financing your own downfall, whether you know it or not."

The next morning, sober and alert, Dan went down to the front desk and was handed an envelope containing the wire transfer. He then went to the dining room and ordered a huge breakfast with coffee.

When he was done, he got the directions to the nearest Westpac Bank and headed over, where he hit the first snag of the day. As he figured, they didn't have enough US cash laying around. The teller told him he could get $500 in Fiji dollars and $1,500 in US$ right then, and it would be another twenty-four hours before she'd be able to honor the rest.

He took the cash that was offered and headed out, back to the hotel.

He pulled out the TO&E that MacDevitt had provided for him and read through it. It read like most other ones of small countries, though this one was a little different. It had tanks.

Where the fuck did they hide the goddamn tanks?

In the eight months he'd been there he'd seen only five tracked vehicles, and those were the tiny Bren Gun Carriers. This document was saying they had five M3 Sherman tanks, two Churchill tanks, two Matilda tanks, and a Japanese tank of unknown armament.

Armor was a game changer. When scrounging the weapons, he'd better make sure he had something to beat a tank. No, not beat a tank, overwhelm it. In this dirty little war there'd be only one chance. No regrouping, no counteroffensives. One shot, win or lose.

Dan didn't plan on losing, so utter destruction and devastation was high on the list.

He knew he'd have to go to Central America and see his contacts face to face for the weapons and ammunition. The sundry other stuff—uniforms, boots, TA50 gear and the like—he could do that right over the phone.

First he ordered a pot of coffee from room service, then made himself two shopping lists. He made calls to Honduras, Guatemala, and Panama, until around 4PM, he'd made his last money transfer to the last Cayman account.

He was pretty pleased with himself at the haul; sans weapons, he had secured enough OG 107s, jungle boots, Alice web gear, and other stuff to completely outfit seven hundred men, not including cargo and static line parachutes and cargo airdrop containers for little more than one hundred grand. He didn't have a shipping address as of yet, so he told his suppliers he'd be back in touch with them in a few days.

He'd also asked, and was getting the runaround about weapons, so he knew he'd still have to go to Central America for that leg. He phoned TWA and booked a flight for Friday afternoon from Nadi to Honolulu, from Honolulu to Mexico City, and from there to Panama City, Panama.

Would Mr. Kruger like first class?

Of course Mr. Kruger would greatly enjoy first class on Nete Ilikimi.

He decided to call it a day and head down to the bar to get some supper. He grabbed his suit coat, room keys, smokes, and headed out. He was pleasantly surprised to bump into Poindexter in the hotel lobby, and he led the way out onto the patio.

When they were both seated, the waiter arrived and took their drink orders.

"Well?" Dan asked when the waiter was gone.

Poindexter replied, "They don't give a shit. I don't know of any other way to tell you."

"What the fuck do you mean they don't give a shit? What about the heroin? What about over half the goddamn island's population in forced labor, into slavery?"

"I don't know what else to say, Kruger. I did try. It's as if—"

"It's not Communism, it's not in their backyard, it's an insignificant piece of real estate that no one ever heard of before. So insignificant, they even bypassed it during World War II and left it to rot. I could go on with about three dozen more excuses better than those."

"Hey, I'm on your side, really I am. To be honest, I'd love to loan you an entire Marine amphibious task force right now. However, my hands are tied by Washington."

"Funny, it was okay to invade an entire island nation three years ago, and no one had ever heard of Grenada before," Dan spat.

"There were American hostages on Grenada," Poindexter said softly.

"What ever happened to what Jack Kennedy said about bearing any burden, supporting any ally?"

"Long gone, Dan. Look, I took the pleasure of pulling your Army and Agency files. You're one of the good guys, or I'd not be here at all. I understand why you left, and what you're trying to do right now. Like I said, they told me to forget about you. You're rogue, a liability, and you're, quote, *going to step on your own dick with golf shoes*, unquote."

"Well, what's done is done. I've still got some contacts back east," Dan said. "So I guess this is it, eh? I'm flying out of here tomorrow, so no worries for you on my part. Have dinner with me. The surf and turf was amazing last night."

After dinner, both men sat facing the harbor. "What about the Aussies?" Dan prompted. "This is their slice of the pie, so to speak."

"I thought about that too, and even had a brief conversation with my counterpart over at the Australian Embassy this morning about it. They're too involved in the crap going on in East Timor right now to worry about some speck in the middle of the ocean."

"That's that, then. One more question for you and we'll call it a night. How well do you know the guys at customs here?"

"Fijian customs? A little, why?"

"I'm going to need a place to ship... stuff. I'm going to be coming into a bunch of stuff that will wind up on Korotonga. I need a safe place to bring stuff in bulk, and then ship it off to parts elsewhere; someplace that if I grease the right wheels with the right lubricant, my stuff will be ignored."

"That I may be able to help you with."

"I'll be in touch. Now I want to bask in the evening twilight and get drunk."

Poindexter stood and shook Dan's hand. "I mean it, I'll do what I can."

"Alright then. Until I'm back in touch with you, probably about a week."

With that, the CIA man walked out of sight through a group of Aussies who were hell-bent on destroying their livers. Dan toasted them silently, and let his gaze drift back towards the harbor.

CHAPTER 7

First class or not, Dan felt like he'd gone six rounds with Muhammad Ali when his last flight landed in Panama City. He had booked ahead from Honolulu for a room at the Best Western, and hailed a taxi when he got through customs and baggage claim.

Partly he was dead tired from the travel, and partly he was dreading seeing the man he would need to see tomorrow. That man was located on the other side of the isthmus, at Ft. Sherman, so he decided to get a room for the night here in Panama City, refresh, recharge his batteries some, and take the bus from here to Christóbal.

It took him the better part of the day to get to the city of Christóbal, across the mouth of the canal, and Limon Bay from Colón and Ft. Sherman, the US Army's Jungle Warfare Training Center. Again, he booked himself into a local hotel, and remembering the phone number, dialed it.

When the Charge Quarters answered on the other end, Dan didn't identify himself, only asked if he could speak to Sergeant Tim Flannery, if he was available.

He waited on the line for a long time, and as he was about to hang up, a familiar voice came on.

"This is Staff Sergeant Flannery. How may I help you?"

"Tim, it's Dan Kruger. I need to talk to you."

After a long pause, the man on the other end of the line hissed, "What makes you think I want to talk to you, you little fuck?"

"Tim, please. This is a little bigger than that. Give me some time this afternoon, hear me out, and if you still hate me, we'll leave it at that and you'll never hear from me again."

"You know," the voice on the other end of the line dropped to a whisper, "I should fucking kill you today and be done with it. I'm pretty sure no one would miss your sorry ass."

"Tim, up until a few months ago, I'd have agreed with you. Something important has come up, and I need your help."

"I'm not going out on any fucked up missions like the last—"

"Tim," Dan cut in, "*OPSEC*. This is not a secure telephone line, besides I'm not in the CIA anymore."

"What?"

"You heard me. I'm no longer with the Agency. I need to talk to you for a few minutes this afternoon. If you don't dig what I've got to tell you, we go our separate ways and you'll never hear from me again."

"Alright," the sergeant on the other end of the line relented. "1700 at Rosa's Café at the corner of Calle 5 and Avenida Amador Guerrero, across from the Catedral Inmaculada Concepión."

"I'll be there," Dan said to a dead handset. He replaced the receiver and checked his watch. He'd have plenty of time to walk there.

His walk took him through several different neighborhoods, and he could feel tension in the air wherever he went. Things had changed here in Panama, and Dan sensed it was not for the better.

He found Rosa's easily, sat down at an empty table al fresco, and waited. An attractive young girl came over to him and asked in Spanish what he would like to drink.

"*Dos Equis, por favor*," he told the smiling girl. She nodded and disappeared into the café, returning quickly with a frosty bottle of the Mexican beer and a pilsner glass. After paying her, he told her in Spanish that he was meeting someone, and they would probably have a late lunch.

Dan sat back and sipped his beer, scanning the avenue from behind dark Wayfarer sunglasses. Flannery should not be too hard to spot. He was a big Irish kid from Philadelphia, 6'2" and 230 pounds like Dan, and even if he wore some sort of disguise, he would stand out like a drag queen at a Mormon funeral.

He didn't have to wait long. Although deeply tanned and as dark as the locals, SSGT Flannery towered above everyone around him, as he would in a country where the average height was 5'3". The severe 'high & tight' military haircut, loud Hawaiian shirt, and the Wayfarer sunglasses rounded out the image of an off-duty American military man in a foreign country.

Flannery locked onto Dan from behind the dark lenses and marched over robotically to Dan's table. Without being invited, the sergeant sat down, placed a folded newspaper on the table in front of him, hand lightly resting on top, and when the waitress appeared, ordered a Miller High Life. He stared silently at Dan for an eternity, fingers now drumming the folded paper until the girl returned with his beer.

Dan quickly paid for it, and Flannery took a long pull from the bottle.

"Sergeant Flannery, it's good to see you. You're looking—"

"It's Staff Sergeant, and it's not good seeing you," the younger man spat.

"Staff Sergeant. Looks like you're on the fast track to Special Forces."

"Enough with the chitchat. What the fuck do you want, Kruger?" Flannery spat, taking a huge pull from his beer, hand never leaving the folded newspaper.

"I need weapons. Rifles, mortars, anti-tank stuff, RGP-7s, Karl Gustavs, whatever I can get my hands on. Enough to arm a battalion."

The sergeant chuckled. "You're not asking for a whole lot. Why not some fucking nukes? They'd be as easy to get around here the way things have been the last year."

"That dried up?" Dan asked, his hopes falling fast. "I've got plenty of money, and I'll pay double."

"Look, even if I wanted to help you, *and I don't*, I couldn't get you a rusty .38 Special with a broken firing pin right now. You can offer triple to every gunrunner from Medellin to Campeche, and it still won't buy you a daisy BB gun."

"Aren't you the bright and rosy ray of sunshine? What the hell happened?"

"I'm not sure of the whole story because it's way above my pay grade, but somehow arms sales went covertly to Iran to get money to fund the Contras down here, and someone found out about it. There's going to be some Congressional hearings in the next year, and they've already got a scapegoat lined up to take the fall, some jarhead light-colonel."

Dan took a pull of his beer and looked out over the busy street crowded with pedestrians. "It appears I'm going to have to look elsewhere."

"Tell me something. If you're not Agency anymore, what the hell do you need the weapons for?"

"Do you plan on shooting me?"

"Not at this time."

"Then put the 1911 away. I know you've got one folded up in the paper, and you've not taken your hand off of it."

"Fair enough," Flannery said, and put the paper down on the empty chair next to him, "But you come here, out of the blue, over a year and half has gone by since your fucked up little foray you had us make up north. We did it, it turned to rancid dog shit, and you left us high and dry, no extraction. We had to fucking walk thirty goddamn clicks to see a friendly face, running gun battle the whole fucking way. Because of you I had to tell my best friend's wife that her husband—the father of their two kids—died in some training accident, and that's why the casket was sealed. Not the truth, that he died in my arms, guts spread over five yards of jungle, his body hastily interred in an unmarked grave. And that she, nor her kids, will ever know that that casket we buried in Sandusky, Ohio was empty save for the one hundred eighty pounds of sandbags."

"Look, Tim—"

"Don't *look, Tim* me goddamn it! You pull that shit, and come here expecting me to fucking trust you? Don't you fucking dare! "

"I deserve that, and more," Dan said in a very small voice. He motioned to the waitress to bring them another round. "If you have a little time, I'll tell you."

"Yeah, I've got time. I'm between girlfriends right now and all I had planned was making shower-babies in the barracks later. Since you got such the fat wallet these days, you're buyin', I'm drinking and listening."

When the girl brought their beer and was out of earshot, Dan began, giving Flannery the whole picture, not merely the Cliff Notes version he gave Poindexter back in Suva. He felt that he owed this man, and to hold back anything wouldn't be right.

After two hours and six beers for each of them, Dan concluded his tale. The sun was low behind the cathedral and the streetlights were coming on. The waitress was scurrying about, lighting candles on the café tables while Dan waited for a reply.

Flannery lit a Winston and contemplated the glowing end for a moment. "If all of that is true, *if* you aren't bullshitting me, that's as fucked up as a soup sandwich."

"Now you know why I need the arms."

"Yeah," Flannery said. "Have you ever thought about cutting out the middle man?"

"Buy direct?"

Flannery shrugged. "Why not?"

"'Oh, hello. May I speak to Mr. Gorbachev? Yes, it's about a large purchase of arms...'"

"Well, maybe not that far. You'd have to go to West Germany. West Berlin in fact," Flannery noted. He pulled a cord from around his neck that had several trinkets on it besides his GI dog tags and tossed it to Dan.

Dan caught it deftly, and inspected it in the dimming light. "What am I looking at here?"

"The rifle round."

"Typical Soviet lacquered steel case, I'm guessing berdan primed. The bullet itself, I've never seen anything like it. Quite a bit smaller than the 7.62mm AK47 or SKS round."

"It's an AK74 round."

"AK74?"

"Yeah, Ivan started replacing the older 47s with the 74s in 1978," Flannery said, becoming animated. "They've now started to trickle over to this side of the pond via Afghanistan and our Mujahedeen brothers."

"So wouldn't it be better if I went to the Middle East?"

"I wouldn't. I think of that place like Br'er Rabbit and the Tar Baby."

"And down here isn't?"

"At least with the Soviets, and the Communists in general, we know who the goddamn enemy is."

"I see your point there. Getting back to the rifle..."

"Oh, yeah. You need to get your hands on the '74. Beats the '47 hands down."

"Why?"

"Well for one, the round itself. It's 5.45mm. Hardly any recoil at all, even less than an M16. It takes the maximum effective range out to about six hundred meters, a lot farther than the '47. It's also about three pounds lighter than the '47, but it's a little longer. The magazine is plastic, and less curved. Basically it's an AK47 from the looks and the reliability viewpoints."

"Lighter rifle and ammo means you can carry more ammo."

"Exactly, and that's why I think the Soviets went with it. Sort of in competition with the M16A1. The best thing on this badass rifle is this funky muzzle break. On full automatic fire, it completely negates all muzzle climb. You can basically keep your sight picture on rock n' roll for a whole magazine."

"No shit. Can't do that with a '47."

"No, you can't. If you want to arm your new troops with the best, get them this rifle."

"Why do I go to West Germany for it?"

"Man, you have been living off the grid for a while. *Glasnost* and *Perestroika* are breaking out all over Eastern Europe and huge chunks of rust are beginning to flake away at the Iron Curtain. Peace is breaking out, and the Soviet Union is running out of money. There's even talk about the Berlin Wall coming down and Germany reuniting before 1990. It's like this. The Soviets got themselves their own little Vietnam to deal with in Afghanistan, and it's bleeding them white. They're out of money. All the troops they have on the western borders in Europe haven't been paid in *months.*"

"Months? Fuck. How'd you come by all of this first-hand knowledge?"

"I got back from the 7th Army NCO Academy in Bad Tolz three weeks ago. Eight weeks TDY in West Germany, including two weeks in West Berlin. My first night in Berlin, me and a few of the guys went to a nightclub. We're not there a half hour and this big bear of a Russian, told me he was a sergeant major, came up to me and asked me if I wanted to buy a T80 tank."

"Get the fuck out of here. A T80?"

"I shit you not. Showed me his ID card to prove his bona fides. Waltzed right in like he owned the place. His name was Yury and he's selling everything that isn't nailed down for cold, hard cash."

"So you think I should go to West Berlin and look this guy up?"

"If you have a laundry list of hardware you need, I think that's the best place for it."

"Easier said than done. Export would be a lot harder than from down here."

"Yury assured me he can get *anything* out of Europe, and that Hamburg is porous."

"Yury, eh? You on a first-name basis with him now?"

"No, nothing like that. I declined the tank, though took him up on a few Tokarev pistols. Shit, who knows? The KGB or the Stasi might have already picked him up."

"Even if they have, from what you've told me, there would be five guys behind him waiting to step into his shoes."

"I agree."

For the first time that evening, Dan felt he could relax. It was full dark now, and the night, although sultry, was bearable.

"I didn't know it was getting that bad behind the curtain. Okay, I'll head to Berlin."

"You do that. And Cap'n?"

"Yeah?"

"I do wish you luck. You pull this off, and you've partly atoned yourself in my book."

"Thank you, Tim."

"In some perverse way, I wouldn't mind being on this mission."

"I think the only mission you should worry about right now is the fact that our waitress hasn't been able to take her eyes off of you all evening."

"No shit?" Flannery smiled, standing up. Dan followed and to his surprise, Flannery held out his hand.

Dan took the firm grip in his. "Like I said, you won't be hearing from me again."

"The world better have ended and I'm president of the US if that happens," Flannery said flatly, and went to hunt down the waitress.

Dan dropped a few hundred pesos on the table to cover the tab, and walked off into the night in the direction of his hotel room.

He was feeling a good buzz from all the beer he'd drank, his stomach rumbling to let him know it was well past his supper time. He made it back to his hotel easily, and found that they served room service all night. He kicked off his shoes, flopped down on the bed, and scanned through the room service menu.

He ordered beef empanadas, a pastry filled with beef, cheese, potatoes, and vegetables, and sancocho, an extremely popular local stew made with chicken vegetables, tomatoes, and coriander, and a six pack of the local beer, Balboa, that he didn't need.

While he waited, he dug through his battered suitcase, and found the stack of 'legend' passports and IDs he still had, and rifled through the short stack until he found what he was looking for.

A West German passport that was still valid for four years, issued to one Heinrich Albrecht, 49 Nettlebeckstraße, West Berlin, Federal Republic of Germany, occupation, Import/Export.

How apt.

A light rapping on the door signaled his food had arrived, and his stomach rumbled in anticipation. A stout waiter pushing a trolley came through the door when Dan opened it, and perfunctorily placed the dishes on the table, then placed the beer in the mini refrigerator. Dan tipped him twenty US dollars, and the man's eyes bulged, a huge grin splitting his face in two. As quickly as the waiter came, he was gone, and Dan sat down at the table and devoured his meal.

After he was done, he grabbed a beer from the fridge and sat down on the bed, reaching for the phone. Dialing the hotel operator, he requested to be connected with the Lufthansa international booking number.

It rang a few times, and when it was answered by a woman named Helga, he spoke in perfect German, with a Berlin accent. *"Guten Abend. Ich würde gerne einen Flug nach Berlin Tempelhof Buchen bitte."*

Good evening. I'd like to book a flight to Berlin, please.

He waited a few moments, and hearing the soft keystrokes of a professional typist on the other end, and then Helga was back with him. *"Ich habe ein Flug morgen früh um 11, Panama City, Berlin über Miami."*

One flight tomorrow, 11AM, Panama City, to Miami, then Berlin.

"Dass wird gut. Gibt es first class zur Verfügung?"

He waited a few moments again, and found that indeed there were first class seats on both legs of his journey tomorrow, and booked one. He thanked her, and after he told her no, there wasn't anything else she could do for him, hung up the receiver. He leaned back on the bed, grabbed the TV remote and, it to a mindless Spanish language *telenovella*, phoned the front desk to place a wakeup call for 6AM, and was fast asleep within minutes.

CHAPTER 8

Dan's flight into Tempelhof was fifteen minutes early, and after retrieving his luggage, he breezed through customs with the fake passport without so much as a hiccup.

He walked out to the taxi stand and found one straightaway, hopped in, and told the driver to take him to the Berlin Hotel, *Lützowplatz* 17. He had a Berlin address. After that, his 'legend' wore thin. He had never been inside that apartment block.

He thought of a quick cover story as to allay suspicion why he was a local staying in a hotel for a few weeks. After his taxi dropped him off, he walked into the lobby up to the front desk, and with a hopeful look, asked if they had any rooms, because, you see, he had returned from a business trip to South America, and found that a burst pipe had flooded his apartment.

The hotel staff was quite accommodating, even giving Dan a suite for the single price. He put it all on Heinrich Albrecht's AMEX with a smile. After making his way to his room, he settled in for a long, body-clock resetting nap. Over the last few days, he had traveled halfway around the world, and it was rapidly catching up to him.

He did not like that the hotel was not close to the nightclub district, and being the middle of winter he could not walk. That, and there were quite a few nightclubs, though he did not recall Flannery being forthcoming with the name of the place where he had met Yury.

He would have to figure it out on his own. He still had plenty of time, and all of the best nightclubs, bars, and discotheques stayed open 24/7 here in Berlin anyway. Therefore, after a long, hot shower, he crawled into bed and drifted off into a deep, dreamless sleep.

Now, five days later, standing outside Club 45, he stood within shouting distance to Checkpoint Charlie on *Wilhelmstraße* smoking an HB cigarette in a late evening snow. He already had a headache from the pounding beats of the dance music the GIs and the local German kids liked, and he steeled himself for the assault on his ears.

He was growing frustrated. He had lost count of the nightclubs and discos he searched, and even asked around at some of them until people began to think he was Stasi, so he backed off some.

There was no door attendant at the entrance, so he pushed in through a mass of teenagers and stepped into the dark interior. A post-modern electronic beat pumped out of the club's speakers, as the singer named Frankie on the recording was telling everyone to *relax, don't do it!*

Dan shouted at the bartender for a Doppel Bock. He took a swig of the cold beer and broke out into a sweat; the club's interior was stifling compared to the sub-freezing air outside. He peered out over the pulsing, dancing crowd and through the thick haze of tobacco, and other *herbal* smoke, scanning the faces for a few moments until...

There!

Sitting in a booth at the back of the club was a large, bald white guy, holding court. He had two other men with him wearing cheap leather jackets and sporting bad institutional haircuts. They *had* to be Soviet Army.

Although it took some time, Dan was able to make his way through the crowd and up to the table.

"*Pardon, di Yury?*" *Pardon, are you Yury?* Dan asked in flawless Russian.

"*Da.* I am Yury," the man replied in thickly accented English.

"I am Heinrich Albrecht. I believe a close associate of mine did business with you recently, and I wish to do even more business with you," Dan said in English, with a German accent, and he felt rather silly.

"What business would that be, Herr Albrecht?"

"I wish to procure a sizable amount of military equipment, including some armored vehicles. I was told that this was possible, is it not?"

Yury let out a huge belly laugh, his face split into a wide grin showing poor dental hygiene. "I deal in cash, and in American dollars only, no exceptions."

"That is acceptable, *Herr?*"

"Busarov. Please, let us go somewhere quieter where we can talk. Follow my associates and I will be along shortly."

Against his better judgment, Dan followed the pair of no-necked strong-arms out towards the back of the bar, passing the unisex restrooms to a dimly lit exit. One stood to the side and held open the door, letting the first one pass, followed by Dan, out into a dark alleyway that smelled of stale human urine and feces.

The exit door slammed shut, the Russian thug who held the door came up behind him, and so quickly he couldn't defend himself, slammed a heavy linen sack over Dan's head. The first one punched him hard, repeatedly in the face, and kicked him as hard as he could in the scrotum. Dan fell to his knees and passed out from the excruciating pain in his groin.

He awoke later, arms bound behind his back, hood still over his head. He was lying on something cold and hard, and he could smell damp concrete. When he tried to sit up the pain in his scrotum was still unbearable, and he let out a muffled groan.

"Ah, Dasha! Our Stasi guest has awakened!" Yury uttered in Russian.

"I'm not Stasi!" Dan shouted back in Yury's native tongue.

"Oh, so you speak Russian also? You may even be KGB."

"I'm not—!" Dan was cut off by a stiff boot into his kidney.

"Did you find anything on him?" Yury asked.

"*Da Tovarisch.* A West German passport under the name Heinrich Albrecht, about one hundred thirty deutschmarks, a pack of HB cigarettes, gold lighter, and this," the man called Dasha said, handing over a handwritten loose-leaf sheet of paper.

Yury took it and began reading. When he was not half finished, began to laugh loudly.

"It looks like the Stasi or the KGB is looking to start a war, Dasha. One thousand AK74s! Six thousand magazines! A half a million rounds of ammunition!"

"Look, I'm not Stasi, not KGB. I'm an American and want to do a little business!" Dan shouted in English from behind the linen hood.

"Oh, now you are CIA?" Yury asked mirthfully.

"No, I'm not CIA. I'm a businessman."

"Dasha, look in the man's mouth and let's see what his teeth tell us, eh?"

Dan was roughly dragged to a sitting position and hood yanked off, still blinded by bright lights. Strong hands forced his mouth open and a second bright flashlight was shoved in his face.

He could smell Dasha's halitosis as his head was turned this way and that, shoving him roughly away when he was done his dental exam.

"*Da.* Silver and amalgam fillings, *Tovarisch.*"

"Stand our guest up, Dasha, and take him to my office."

Dasha grabbed Dan under the armpit, and still tied up, forced him to walk down a dark corridor towards a lighted room at the end.

A modestly appointed office was set up, and Dan was shoved unceremoniously into a padded seat that faced the desk, leaving him alone. After a moment, a side door to the office opened, and Yury strode in unaccompanied. Frowning at seeing Dan still tied up, he produced a pocketknife and cut the ropes that bound his wrists.

"Allow me to introduce myself. I am *Starshina*, or Sergeant Major Yury Busarov, 3rd Soviet Red Banner Combined Arms Army."

The big man sat down at his desk, placed his elbows on the blotter, and touched his fingertips together. "What am I going to do with you, mystery man?" Yury asked rhetorically.

"I'd hope we'd still be able to do business, Yury."

"How do you know I even want to do business with you?"

"I know with Gorbachev's new policies, you haven't been paid in quite some time. You and your men are in need of cold, hard cash, and that, *Tovarisch,* I have plenty of."

"Yes, with *Perestroika* and *Glasnost,* things have not been all that great for us here. You say you have cash. This list you have, it will be very expensive. How do I know you have that much cash?"

"How much cash are we talking about, Yury?"

"American dollars?"

"Yes, greenbacks."

"I will have to figure this all out, *Herr...?*"

"Herr Albrecht," Dan said.

"Yes, Herr Albrecht. One must remain in legend. Glancing at your list, the T80s, they are possible, and will be the most expensive item on your list," Yury said, letting it hang out there as a giant question mark floating between them.

"I said before, money is no object. How much?"

"Five million each."

"Done," Dan said without hesitation, and Yury blinked. "I want ten full combat loads for both, with an option for two hundred more combat loads in the future."

"And the rest?"

"New, never been fired, or as close to that as possible."

"All the ammunition, mortars, grenades... this item here, Herr Albrecht, one thousand RDG5 hand grenades. May I suggest the RGO grenade? A newer model, and far more reliable."

"Now there's the Yury I expected, salesman, not thug."

"I apologize for the rough handling, Herr Albrecht. It was business, nothing personal."

"Apology accepted. What are your terms?"

"After I know for sure you can come up with this kind of money, I will say half up front and the other half on delivery. Will there be a need to export the items out of Europe?"

"Yes. I will need assistance with the shipping."

"Where? I will not be able to go ahead with the sale if they are to be used against my fellow Socialist comrades, Herr Albrecht."

"That I will let you know after the delivery, but I can assure you, Yury, they won't be used against your Socialist comrades. Also, I shouldn't have to add everything must be disguised."

"I assumed as much. I will obtain a ride home for you this evening. Tell me where you are staying."

Dan gave him the name and address of his hotel in West Berlin. "Yury, I know you said this was business, not personal, but I will add one caveat to our deal."

"And that is?"

"If your goon Dasha gets near me one more time, I'll kill him."

"I see."

"I've been knocked around a little too much in the last few weeks, and it's wearing thin."

"Noted."

"Now if you don't mind, the ride home?"

"Simples. I will drive you there myself."

Yury led Dan out of the warehouse, Dasha and the other goon nowhere to be seen. They walked halfway up the block to a nondescript Opel sedan and Yury squeezed behind the wheel.

Once they were on their way, Dan realized with a start that they were in East Berlin. He was all of a sudden very nervous, and he told his companion.

"Ah! Do not worry, Herr Albrecht. It is a piece of pie! Simples!"

"Don't you mean cake?" Dan said as they lined up in the queue at Checkpoint Charlie, the gateway back to the West.

"Cake, pie all the same!"

When they pulled up to the guard house, a US Army Sp4 walked up to the driver's side and asked Yury what his business was.

"Hello, Frank," Yury greeted the guard jovially. "I am taking my Capitalist comrade Herr Albrecht back home. He had a late night and he's had far too much vodka."

"Sure thing, Yury. Oh, and the wife loved those nesting dolls," the Sp4 said with a wide grin and casually waved them into West Berlin.

"See? What did I tell you? Simples!"

"Okay, Yury, okay," Dan said, letting out a sigh of relief.

Yury tried to make small talk all the way to Dan's hotel, fishing for information of the true identity of Herr Albrecht without much luck. The only thing he did get out of Dan was he was ex-US Army, and a veteran of Vietnam.

It was then, as Yury pulled up to the front of Dan's hotel it struck him, he had not asked once for directions. Yury told Dan not to stray far from his hotel, as he would be in contact with him in a day or two with the details. The bastard knew his way around West Berlin like a native.

Hopping out of the Opel into the sub-freezing air, Dan hobbled to the lobby of his hotel, and made it to the elevators without being seen by the night concierge. The lobby was overheated, and going from one extreme to the other, Dan broke out into a sweat waiting for the double doors to open.

The ride to his floor was a quick one, and as soon as he was in his suite, he turned on the TV to CNN, stripped, and ran a hot bath. While the tub was filling, he went to the wet bar and poured himself a healthy snort of schnapps.

Naked, he walked to the tub and tested the water and finding it satisfactory, turned the taps off and lowered himself into the steaming water. Taking a sip of the schnapps, he leaned back, letting the hot water ease the pain of the beating he had taken from Yury's man earlier and the thought angered him.

He would not let his guard down with Yury again, business or no business.

He turned into a hermit the next few days, only venturing down to the lobby and restaurant to eat and buy more cigarettes. On the afternoon of the third day, Dan lay on top of the made bed, dozing to the International sports scores on CNN when a heavy rap on his suite's door awakened him.

Getting up in a flash, Dan grabbed his Browning High-Power, and hiding it behind his torso in his right hand, opened the door a crack. He peered out, only to see the hulking form of Yury engulfing the entire corridor outside his room.

Dan opened the door and ushered the big Russian inside, locking it after he closed the door behind them. Yury strutted across the suite to a large, overstuffed sofa, and plopped down unceremoniously, spreading his beefy arms across the back.

"Please come in and make yourself at home," Dan muttered as an afterthought of sarcasm. He went to the wet bar. "Anything to drink?"

"I will take a Jack Daniels and Coca-Cola, please."

Dan poured the mix into a rocks glass, and made himself a gin and tonic. Handing the Jack and coke to Yury, he sat down and lit an HB cigarette, blew out a cloud of blue smoke and asked, "Well?"

"Herr Albrecht. I can get you everything on your shopping list, delivery in three days from today."

"The price?"

"Thirty million US dollars. Half now to expedite your order, and the other half upon delivery."

Dan nearly choked at the amount, somehow managing to keep himself cool and collected. "Do you have a Swiss account?"

"Yes, I do, I do indeed. Here is the number if you are going to wire the money now," the Russian said, handing Dan a plain white business card that simply stated Yury's name, the title "Proprietor", surprisingly, a West German phone number, and when Dan turned it over, saw the words Bank Suisse, and a ten-digit number.

Dan walked over to the phone, dialed the number from memory, and in German, ordered the wire transfer of $15 million, USC into Yury's account. When that was completed, he returned to the easy chair across from the big Russian, and sipped his adult beverage. Setting the glass down, he said, "You may want to wait about fifteen minutes and call your bank to make sure the money is there."

"*Tovarisch* Albrecht, I trust you."

"That's funny, because I don't trust you."

"To be expected. Now, back to business. I'm going to assume the money is there right now. Where would you like the merchandise to be delivered to?"

"I can give you an exact place in a few days, Yury."

"It is simples. Not to worry, *Tovarisch*. I have warehouses that we can get the items to."

"What about the shipping? What you quoted me the other day and the quote today is quite different. I'll assume that shipping is now included?"

"Of course. Consider it, how would you say, a bulk-order discount?" Yury said with slight hesitation "For that, I will need a destination."

"Now?"

"*Da*. Now, comrade."

"Alright," Dan said, giving it all away in one monumental leap of faith in this big Russian, "Suva, Republic of Fiji."

"Simples. Now, the T80s. They are too big to ship in the shipping containers. Are there end-users there that might expect huge pieces of machinery, or better yet, customs won't be phased by huge machinery arriving?"

"Yes, Hydro-Electric works on Korotonga, not too far away. Suva would be the largest, closest port to there. And the BRDMs?"

"They slide right into a twenty foot container like they were made to fit." Yury broke into a huge, broken-toothed grin. The big man finished his drink, stood, and held out his hand. Dan took the beefy hand in his. "It is nice doing business with you. Now I will go and check to see if the money is in my bank. If it is, you will receive a phone call from me personally tomorrow morning. It is then I will give you the name and address of a good warehouse where we will meet, and where we will finalize the deal."

Dan showed Yury to the door, and the Russian headed down to the lobby where he found a bank of phone booths. Selecting the farthest from the hotel's front desk, he entered and dialed the International Toll Free number from memory. After entering the numbers requested by the automated phone system, he received his answer.

He hung up the receiver and quickly exited the hotel, getting in the back of the Opel sedan he drove the night before, only this time was being chauffeured by Dasha. When the door was shut, the young Russian sped off into the West Berlin traffic.

"Dasha," Yury said, "you and I will never have to work again after these next few days."

"So this American who is not CIA is telling the truth?"

"Yes, Dasha, he is," Yury said, hearing again the automated phone recording telling him that he now had more money in his bank account than he'd ever dreamed of having, and that soon will double yet again. He must remember this American, respect him as a close business associate, and remind Dasha on the old parable of The Golden Goose, and how not to kill it.

With that though, he thought deeper on how to conceal his growing wealth and business from both the Stasi and the KGB long enough to survive the impending implosion of the Soviet Union.

◆◆◆◆◆◆

Dan was startled awake by the ringing of the telephone in the early morning hours.

"Hallo?"

"Herr Albrecht?"

"*Ja. Wer ist das?*" Who is this?

"Yury, *Commeraden,*" the Russian spoke in German, then switched to English. "Three days from now. Warehouse 72, number 12 Schlenzigstraße, off of Harburger Chaussee, the port of Hamburg."

"Alright, got it," Dan said into a dead receiver. He turned on the bedside lamp and looked at his wristwatch. 5AM. He sprang to life, taking a shower, getting dressed, and throwing some things together in a small case for a few nights away.

As he knotted his tie in the bathroom mirror, he thought about Yury, and the balls he must possess to even contemplate what he was doing. If Yury were caught, he would have a very short trial and an even shorter walk to a brick-paved interior courtyard of Lubyanka Prison off Lubyanka Square in downtown Moscow, a 9mm bullet to the back of his head, and a shallow and unmarked grave.

On the other hand, if he got away with it, Yury was now one rich motherfucker, and Dan was the one who put him there. He was unsure whether it was a good thing or a bad thing, whether he had created a monster or not, when he sat down in his usual table at the hotel's restaurant and ordered a typical German breakfast of a single soft-boiled egg, black bread, and cold cuts and sausages.

Once finished with breakfast, he took his coffee to the hotel lobby, ordered a hired car for a few days with the concierge, and he sipped the brew while reading the newspaper.

It was not quite 8AM when a neatly dressed teenager entered the lobby and called out for Herr Albrecht. Dan called the boy over, and was handed the keys to a 1986 Audi Quattro and a map of West Germany. He thanked the boy and tipped him ten deutschmarks.

Tossing his case into the trunk, he slid behind the wheel, started the engine, and opened the map. Berlin to Hamburg should only take about three hours on the Autobahn 24, so he steered in that direction.

Once on the open highway, he let the horses run. He loved driving the Autobahn. Well before lunch, he made it to Hamburg, and found the warehouse that Yury had told him to go after a brief search.

He drove around casing the place, and when he was satisfied, he left to find a hotel, and located one only a few kilometers away. A little run-down, but it was cheap, nondescript, and had a restaurant. The *hausfrau* was a little bit huffy and short with him when he said he did not have a reservation. However, from the looks of the empty parking lot outside, he was sure he could probably have his pick of rooms.

The last thing he did was look in the phone directory, and found a close by sporting goods store and in a short fifteen minutes, walked to the place, purchased a good pair of Zeiss binoculars and a two quart vacuum thermos, and wandered back to the motel.

CHAPTER 9

Dan had found a decent place to park about a block away from the warehouse where he could stake it out for a few days. Although it would have been nice if he had one more person so he could watch it twenty-four hours a day, he simply adapted to what he could realistically do, and settled for a day shift stakeout.

With all the comings and goings of trucks laden with shipping containers, he was well hidden down the block. The first day and a half was boring, then he noticed some activity around noon the second day.

A familiar Opel sedan arrived, followed soon after by a dozen trucks loaded with shipping containers marked Maersk or Hamburg Süd, along with a few regular tractor-trailers branded with a local appliance store logo.

Dan gave it one more day, and on the middle of the third day, feeling increasingly cramped, he drove off down the road towards the warehouse. Before he could drive into the industrial complex, a German compact car with a flashing amber light cut him off and blocked his way. The small car had a banner in the front, which read in German and English "Caution! Wide Load."

A large Mercedes truck rounded the corner then, towing a lowboy trailer with a massive rectangular shaped wooden crate securely chained to the bed. Stenciled in huge black letters on the crate was "Siemens Hydro." Dan had to smile. He would give the big Russian points for creativity.

A second truck followed the first, along with the similar trailing car with flashing amber lights, and when clear, Dan followed on behind until he was stopped at the large rolling doors to the warehouse by a man in overalls and not an ounce of humor.

"Where are you going?" the man asked in broken German. Looking past him into the shadows of the warehouse Dan saw another guard, this one holding a Krinkov machine gun at the ready.

"In there, this is my shit you're unloading," Dan said, trying to keep a smile on his face.

The familiar bear shaped Yury came out of the warehouse. He called to the man in Russian, who quickly backed away and waved Dan forward.

Once inside the vast building, Dan stopped his rental car and got out as the automatic rolling doors slowly closed. He walked directly over to Yury, who greeted him with a suffocating bear hug and a slap on the back that threatened to knock the wind out of Dan.

"Ah, Herr Albrecht. Let me show you what we're doing." Yury dragged Dan over to where a huge forklift was busy lifting all of the shipping containers off their trucks and placing them in a row along the vast warehouse floor.

Though the building was far too big for what they needed, several square acres, it did effectively hide what was going on from prying outside eyes. Dan noticed that some of the containers were empty, some were full to the brim as Yury's men began opening them up.

"What's the story there?"

"Simples! You watch. We take half of each loaded container, and put them into the other empty containers, and then the sugar goes in."

"Sugar?"

"*Da*, come with me!" Yury led Dan over to the closest twenty foot shipping container. It had already been stripped of half its contents, and Dan walked in to inspect what was in them. Yury sensed what he wanted, and handed him a crowbar.

Dan took it and cracked open a random wooden crate to find one of the ten NVS/DShK 12.7mm heavy machine guns he'd asked for. Yury's men stopped what they were doing and let Dan walk through each container, checking with his list.

At the end, Dan looked at Yury and smiled. "I've got to hand it to you, you've managed to get everything on my list."

"Even the T80s. We did have to remove the main gun tubes so as not to look so obvious. I have the instructions written in English on how to reinstall them quickly once they get where they need to go."

"Siemens Hydro. You're a goddamn genius."

"I know. I frighten myself sometimes."

"So, this sugar. What did you mean by that?"

Yury pointed to one of the local appliance store trucks, where a forklift was busy unloading the trailer, and loading each of the half-filled shipping containers with brand-new refrigerators, washing machines, console stereos, and color TVs.

"Oh, I get it. Great idea. Any nosey customs agent in Fiji will see those, and will grease his palms also."

"And they're at no extra cost to you, *Tovarisch!*"

"Better not be, for what I'm paying you."

"Speaking of which, I know we are friends now, but business is business, so I would very much like to get paid."

"Where's your office?"

Yury led the way to the front of the vast building, and through a door and up a flight of steep stairs to an office that overlooked the entire operation. He took a seat behind the desk, Dan on a padded chair in front of it. The big Russian opened a drawer, produced a bottle of premium Russian vodka, and placed it on the table.

"Vodka, *Tovarisch?*"

"Why not?" Dan reached over the desktop, grabbed the telephone, and dialed. After waiting to be prompted, he entered more numbers on the keypad, and hung up when he was finished. He fervently hoped that the sheer volume of money in that account would cover the disappearance of a little over thirty million dollars, and that neither Nete Ilikimi or that little troll Tiki would be the wiser.

"There, that should cover it," he said to Yury. "The other fifteen million and I even threw in a cool million for the white goods!"

Yury poured healthy shots of vodka into rocks glasses, and handed one over to Dan. "To a long lasting business relationship!"

"I'll drink to that. You never know when I might need some more hardware."

"Good, good!"

"There is one thing though, and it's of no consequence you didn't deliver it. It's the cargo parachutes and airdrop containers, Yury. I didn't see them, and if they're not there, it'll make me have to rethink my entire operational plans..." Dan had doubled up on those. He'd gotten them from his Central American contact also, yet wanted more in case Joey Sutcliffe needed to make more trips with the C47.

Yury's face split into a grin, erasing the worried look he'd had moments before, "Herr Albrecht, they are packed in the wooden crates with the tanks. If anyone should happen to peer into the cracks in the wood, they'll see what looks like lengths of pipe, to go along with the hydroelectric equipment, not a top of the line Soviet main battle tank!"

Dan hoisted his glass. "*Nastrovia!*" He downed half of the clear liquid in one gulp, as did Yury.

"Yury, I must ask this now. The men you have down there working right now, you will pay them, won't you?"

"Of course I will pay them. Handsomely!" Yury boasted with a hurt look on his face.

"I'm glad to hear that. Because I'd hate to find out our newly found friendship was based merely on greed."

"Well, *Tovarisch*, it is," Yury laughed. "I also have always taken care of my men."

"I'm happy to hear that. One final thing..."

"Yes?"

"How did you get this amount of materiel out of the Soviet army's camp in East Berlin, through West Berlin, across West Germany to Hamburg in broad daylight without being seen?"

"Herr Albrecht, it's all in the greasing of palms. I pay people off to look the other way. Simples!"

"Simples, eh?"

"Now for the details, Comrade." The big man pulled out a briefcase and opened it in his lap. He had a huge pile of papers in his hand, and placed them on his desk, pushing aside the briefcase. "These are the export papers, end-user papers, and shipping invoices. All the weights will be correct, shipping container numbers will match the manifests. All will be in order. Also, all the weapons and materiel will be on a separate manifest, one that only you will have, again, matching up each item or items with its container number. The only other thing I need from you, Herr Albrecht, is the end-user. Who are we shipping this stuff to?"

"The tanks, I mean the Hydro Electric stuff, directly to me. Herr Heinrich Albrecht, Siemens Hydro, Suva, Fiji, care of the Government of Korotonga, Republic of."

"And the other containers?"

"How many will there be in total?"

"Looks like thirty standard 20-foot shipping containers."

Dan laughed a little inside. "Send those to Johnsons Hardware & White Goods, Suva, Fiji, Republic of, Care of M. Poindexter, Proprietor."

Good old Poindexter is going to absolutely shit when he sees this shipment, Dan mused.

"Herr Albrecht, you do not understand. The EUC, or End User Certificate must state that that person or government will not transfer the arms yet again to a third party."

"We're smuggling them out in the first place."

"If the UN gets information on a shipment of brand new Soviet military hardware showing up in the South Pacific, it will raise many red flags, and open up many ways that lead right back to me if proper End-User Certificates are not used."

"So basically you need a person representing the government where the guns will end up to say *'yeppers, they're all for us, we're not taking them anywhere else for resale.'* Is that what you mean?"

"*Da Tovarisch.* It is very important, especially with this amount of arms and equipment."

"Okay. President Taito Yasi, Korotonga, Republic of, for modernizing its defense force," Dan said, thinking it utterly ridiculous having to have proper paperwork on shit he was buying illegally and smuggling halfway across the globe, violating dozens of international laws.

"That will do nicely."

It took the better part of the rest of the day for Yury's men to unload, then reload all of the shipping containers, getting the weights and balances correct, and all the paperwork in order, including Dan's 'secret' manifest. Dan and Yury left the work to Yury's men and the two men walked down the street to a *gasthous* for a long lunch.

As the last truck left the warehouse, the sun was sinking below the western horizon. Dan and Yury walked out of the huge rolling doors. "I guess this is it then."

"*Da.* One last thing. Here are the ships the cargo is going on, and dates of arrival."

Dan took the offered paper and read aloud, "Hamburg Süd Lines Columbus Australia, arriving Suva, Fiji, Republic of, on or around the 19th of April, and the Hamburg Süd Lines C/V

Antares arriving same, on or about the 25th of April. They're a good ninety days out. Why two ships?"

"Because the containers now go on container ships. That's all they haul. Other bulkier freight goes on standard cargo vessels."

"Got ya. That card you gave me, does the phone number on it reach you?"

"*Da*, it is an answering service in West Berlin. It is how you can get in touch with me, Herr Albrecht."

"Okay then, I'll bid you a goodbye. It's been a pleasure doing business with you."

"Same here, Heinrich."

Dan slid behind the wheel of his rented Audi and headed off back in the direction of Berlin. Three hours later, he was ensconced in his hotel room. He first ordered room service and checked his wristwatch.

Doing a little arithmetic, he calculated the time difference between there and Korotonga, and dialed the number by memory. It only rang twice, and a familiar Scottish brogue answered.

"Neville, it's Dan. How are things in the tropical paradise?"

"Ach, laddie we've missed you! How's yer' old man?"

"Sadly, he died. I'll be back to work in a few days."

"No worries. Anything else ye might be able to tell me?"

"Yes, I did a fuck-ton of shopping when I was here."

"Aye, did ye now? Did ye get everything ye be lookin' fer?"

"That I did, Neville."

"That is splendid news then. I'll let the men know ye be back in a few days, and I'll get hold of that scoundrel Sutcliffe to expect a call from ye."

"As soon as I book my reservations for the flight back, I'll give him a call."

"You do that, laddie."

"We're going to need him too."

"Too true, laddie. Now shut yer geggie and get off the phone. I'll meet you at the airport when you get here."

"Wilco, out." Dan hung up the phone and a rap at the door announced his room service dinner.

He ate while watching CNN, and when he was done, called Lufthansa and reserved a first class flight direct from Tempelhof to LaGuardia in New York City at 10AM tomorrow.

That flight was on time and arrived at LaGuardia at 10PM. He breezed through customs as Heinrich Albrecht. As soon as he was clear of the baggage area, he ducked into a men's room, and into one of the stalls.

Taking his carry-on bag, he dug through until he had found his real, or Daniel Kruger, passport. He would slip back into his old self for the remainder of this trip back to Korotonga.

At the departures lounge, he found a pretty blonde-haired woman unoccupied at a Continental Airlines desk and approached her with his best smile.

"Good evening, how may I help you?" she asked.

"I hope you can. It's a sudden business trip, I found out thirty minutes ago. I hope my secretary was able to make the reservations," Dan said hopefully, lacing a little worry into his voice for good measure.

"May I see your passport, Mr...?"

"Kruger. Dan Kruger. Here it is," Dan replied, handing over his battered US passport.

"Where will you be heading to?"

"Nadi, Fiji," he said, not even bothering to mention Korotonga. The less said of the place over the next few months, the better.

"Business or pleasure?" she gushed, blue eyes sparkling.

"Unfortunately just business."

"That's too bad. I've always wanted to go to Fiji. And looking here at my computer, I'm not seeing any reservations."

"Damn!"

"Don't you worry, Mr. Kruger. I'll sort something out for you."

"I'm sure you will, and you can call me Dan," Dan said, looking at her nametag, "Karen."

The girl blushed and went all businesslike on the computer for a few seconds asking, "Coach or first class?"

Dan smiled seductively. "First class."

A few more flicks on her keyboard, and boarding passes began to print to a dot-matrix printer on the girl's desk, as well as an itinerary. When the printer finished, she tore them off and handed them to Dan, along with his passport. He barely noticed her take a pen and scribble something down and put it with his passes.

"Here you go, Mr. Kruger. I've got you a redeye flight departing in an hour to LA, then a connecting flight direct to Nadi with only a two-hour layover in LA."

"You're good, Karen," Dan complimented to which the girl blushed bright red. Dan handed over an AmEx platinum card to pay for the flights.

He strode through the empty terminal, and found that most of the bars and lounges were closed, save for one within earshot of his departure gate for his flight to LA.

He sat on a worn padded barstool, ordered a Miller High Life, and waited for his flight to begin boarding. He decided to look through his papers when a blank boarding pass fell out, with a hasty message written on the back that made him smile.

Karen 212-555-3669

He hadn't lost his touch. He folded the pass and dropped it into his inside jacket pocket and quickly forgot about it.

Both flights were on-time and there were no hassles at either airport. He'd phoned both Joey Sutcliff and MacDevitt from the Continental first class lounge at LAX, and as he'd said he would, Joey had the old C47 parked on the tarmac next to the arrivals terminal at Nadi when he touched down.

MacDevitt had also agreed to meet both men back at Joey's hangar at Kotara upon their arrival and it was there they planned on talking to Joey about joining their loose confederacy.

Dan and Joey made small talk the entire flight back to Korotonga. Joey, not only an exceptional pilot, was an extremely likeable person. Dan hoped that would work in his favor when he and Neville attempted to recruit him upon landing at Kotara.

Coming into the airport, the air was rough as thunderheads were stacking up in the late afternoon heat and humidity. It was coming into the wet season, and afternoon thunderstorms were to be a daily occurrence for the foreseeable future.

Joey taxied the twin engine plane up to the front of his hangar, a mid-war corrugated tin affair that Joey could squeeze the Dakota into, along with his prized Zero, and had an office/living quarters in the rear. The C119 Packet was forced to weather it alongside, heavy green tarpaulin tightly lashed over the cockpit windows to save the interior from the unforgiving tropical sun.

Having traveled for the better part of twenty-four hours, Dan was dead tired. Still, this one last chore before he got any rest had to be taken care of today, or getting the equipment onto the island would be next to impossible. He waved out the window at Neville, who was leaning against a coconut palm in the shade, smoking his pipe. Dan went outside and strode over to MacDevitt, shook his hand, and studied Neville's body language.

Nothing stirred any warning, so Dan relaxed a little. "Good to be back, Nev."

"Good to have you back, laddie. How was the shopping trip?"

"Excellent. I was able to get everything on our list and a whole lot more very interesting toys we can play with."

"You've managed to get all of it?"

"I had to change venues. My original supply channels have dried up. I had to go a lot further east to procure most of the items we require."

"How far east?"

"Let's say some rust rubbed off when I went under a certain curtain."

"No kidding?"

"I shit you not, Sergeant Major. It was an eye-opener, for sure. I have one solid lead for high-end Soviet military gear."

"Until the KGB finds him."

"I'll hope that doesn't happen, because when the stuff gets here, you'll shit."

"You got some armor?" MacDevitt asked, eyes growing wide.

"How's 4 BRDM-2s and 4 T80s sound to you?"

"Bloody hell! Did you say T80? Like in a T80 Main Battle Tank?"

Dan grinned. "I did."

"I'm not even going to ask..."

"How much they cost? Don't. There is one hitch with them."

"What's that?"

"Some assembly required. They had to remove the main gun tube to fit them into the crates to ensure the disguise worked, so we'll have to put them back together ourselves."

"If we can get them onto the island, the poor bastards won't have a chance."

"That's the general idea, Sar' Major. We've got approximately eighty-eight days before shipment arrives to train up the men. Once we've got the rest of the gear, firearms practice, practice with radio procedures, firing the mortars, everything will commence."

"A six-month time frame?"

"Thereabouts."

"So around Independence Day."

"Korotongan independence?"

"Aye. You know how the 'president' loves all that pomp and circumstance."

"Yeah, last year was a real dog & pony show."

"We get Joey to airdrop everything?"

"With the exception of the tanks and BRDMs. He tells me he's got a friend in Suva with an old LST."

"Well then, Captain, let's go and persuade him to join the correct side of an already lost war."

"If you're that certain, Sar' Major."

"I am," MacDevitt said with rock steady finality and led Dan over to a side door of the rusting hangar.

CHAPTER 10

It took all of five minutes to convince Joey, with a promise of the possibility of the new/old president financing a real airline with a few new planes and pilots.

He proved his loyalty over the next fortnight when the first shipment of uniforms, boots, and TA50 gear arrived in Fiji. Joey took three nights and he and Dan, along with Jimenez and the ex-Royal Marine Archie Davis, broke open the shipment, split it up, and packed all of it into the first set of parachuted airdrop containers.

Over those three nights, he successfully airdropped all of the uniforms and equipment onto pre-planned drop zones on Korotonga, flying well out of the way of villages, on instruments only, so no one would ever be the wiser.

Once the weapons and ammunition arrived, he'd take the larger Russian cargo containers and do it all over again with the C119.

With only ten left before the shipments were scheduled to arrive, Dan sat with MacDevitt at 'their' table at the very back of the veranda at the Grand Hotel in Kotara, sipping beer and watching the sun set into the western South Pacific.

Dan and his men had done all they could do to get the uniforms, boots, and web equipment to all of the police officers turned soldiers without any suspicions. They had trained them as well as they could, but could go no further until the arms and ammunition arrived from Europe.

Dan stubbed out his cigarette, downed the last of his beer, and winked at MacDevitt. "It's your shout."

"Aye, that it is," Neville said. He took his and Dan's bottles back to the bar, returning moments later with fresh ones. "So, Dan, you were saying about the placement of the mortars?"

"Yeah, the hill overlooking the palace. From up there we'll be able to drop rounds on their grapes with impunity."

"You know that means a visit to the major."

"I know. I've been putting it off for too long anyway."

"What're your thoughts on him?"

"I'm not sure yet. I have a feeling he's not to be trusted, so I'll probably keep him in the dark."

"Smart move."

"Any thoughts on the T80s?"

"Aye. We've already discussed staging the BRDMs over on Korotona. They're amphibious, and as long as the ocean is nice and smooth, they can easily make the half-mile swim by themselves."

"Agreed."

"The tanks, on the other hand, need help."

"Hence Joey's friend's LST."

"Right. We bring them from Suva and stay over the horizon until we've got them reassembled, and land them on Korotona overnight in the darkness. We'll keep the crews we've picked for that job there, camouflage the whole camp, and train them there."

"I'll be a short training, like only a handful of days. I hope they have a sharp learning curve."

"Soviet equipment is made so even the densest peasant can use it. We'll be fine, as most of these Korotongan cops are pretty savvy. I reckon we leave those there on the far island, and before sunup on D-Day, all four of the BRDMs come ashore. The first one stops here on the south side of the bridge and disembarks its squad of infantry to hold the bridge from any assault from the palace. One goes overland to meet up with the men from the eastern police station, and those men will assault the army barracks there."

"After we cut the phone lines."

"Aye."

"The other two?"

"They go north and south, and do the same thing. Link up with the coppers/infantry and assault the north/south army barracks right at sunrise. As soon as the BRDMs are ashore and on their missions, it'll be time for the LST to come into the harbor, nose up to the beach on this side of the Kota River, and offload the tanks and about two companies worth of men."

"All well and good, until something happens and we lose the south side of the bridge."

"We won't lose the bridge."

"You're that sure?"

"Laddie, methinks the first time these clowns in the World War II uniforms and their bolt-action rifles get sight of the BRDMs, let alone the tanks, they'll shit their collective trousers and run back into the palace compound."

"Alright. Say by D-Day plus one hour, we've got the palace surrounded, a beachhead and bridgehead here, and have if not completely subdued the army barracks on the other side of the island, we've got them in a position where they've been neutralized."

"Correct."

"So far, so good."

"Then you and I take the Land Rovers I'll squirrel away behind the pub, take the mortar men and their weapons and ammo up to the major's house. Once there, we set the tubes up, and immediately start dropping mortar bombs on their melons. Once the mortars are set up and firing, you and I leave it under the chief of police's control, and head up the mountain and meet up with the rest of our lads who've abandoned their posts overnight, and using the escape route you found in the bougainvillea, make their way to a rally point in the jungle, bringing along President Yasi."

"Where we go to the radio station, take it over, and let President Yasi speak to his people."

"It'll be a mop-up after that."

"The radio station will be the toughest nut to crack. Two companies, you said?"

"At last recon. And several .303 Vickers machine guns."

"Wonderful. He must not want anything to happen to that radio station."

"I'd say. It's guarded as strongly as the mine. It's why I wanted our men on it, not the green troops. All of us, to a man, has seen real live combat on the two-way rifle range."

"Enough said, Sar' Major."

"Once we have the president making his broadcast, Ilikimi will have very few choices indeed, that is if he's still alive," MacDevitt said. "Besides, we don't want to show that the coup was in any way influenced by outside sources."

"How do you plan on doing that?"

"I hope you don't mind, Dan. When you told me to come up with a plan and run with it, I took it upon myself to put into motion a few of my own personal twists."

"What you've come up with so far is simple and brilliant. Personal twists? Like what?"

"Again, if I overstepped my bounds, I apologize."

"Just tell me what you've got cooking."

"My cousin Zara will be arriving a few days before the celebrations for Independence Day. She's a reporter from the *New Zealand Herald*. She and a photographer will be arriving to cover the celebrations."

"And she gets the scoop on the overthrow of Nete Ilikimi, and the subsequent discovery of the heroin factory and all of its splendid little Nazi-esque horrors."

"Exactly."

"Nothing like throwing a little nepotism into the mix." Dan guffawed. "Tell me, does she know there's going to be a coup?"

"Nae. I didn't let on a thing. Simply wrote her a letter telling how beautiful it was here, and such hidden jewel so to speak, and how she should come up for a visit, and how about right around the island's celebrations?"

"Sly fuck, you."

"That I am. Anyway, she wrote back right away, saying that there wasn't much going on in Auckland at the moment, and it'd be great to catch up."

Dan went to the bar, this time bringing back a bucket filled with ice and an entire six-pack. He plopped it down unceremoniously, pulled a bottle of Miller High Life out, and twisted off the top.

"Here's to the best laid plans." He held the bottle up as a salute, taking a long pull.

MacDevitt agreed and grabbed his own bottle of beer. "Here, here!" There were not a whole lot of people in the place tonight. Each night the crowd looked thinner and thinner, and the inside looks people had, the looks that one kept hidden behind a cheery, wide smile, were those of fear and terror.

The locals were getting sparser and sparser, and things were coming to a head, all because of one man's greed. Dan ran the plan over and over again in his mind and it seemed flawless.

However, most plans look flawless on paper. Once the first round was fired, and sometimes even well before that, plans could rapidly turn to shit. He hoped, maybe, this plan wouldn't go to shit. It had to work. It was, what had said in Hamburg?

Simples!

Dan leaned back in his chair and propped both jungle-booted feet up on the veranda railing, mulling things over in his head. The tide had come up with the setting of the sun, and the waves lapped at the wooden pilings.

"Did I miss anything?" MacDevitt asked in the darkness.

"Air support. I'd love to have some of that."

"We might have some," MacDevitt said.

The pair was interrupted then by a Melanesian waitress who brought a lighted candle in a glass jar, and a lighted mosquito coil. While the rains in the afternoon cooled off the oppressive heat and humidity, it also brought huge black swarms of the little bastards.

"How?" Dan asked as soon as the waitress was out of earshot.

"Joey's Zero. He's got enough ammo for a full load of both the twin machine guns in the nose, and also the two 20mm cannons in the wings. He says it'll give him two or three passes over the palace, and he's toying with the idea of making up some napalm to drop on the factory."

"No napalm, not on the factory. Too many innocent civilians there held hostage. Ironically, that will be the safest place for them the minute the rounds start to fly."

"You're okay with him strafing the place?"

"Sure. Any bit of surprise we can throw at them, the better."

"Agreed."

"I for one, can't wait to see that."

"Me too. As long as he can shoot straight," Dan added soberly.

"So now what?"

"We wait, Sar' Major. We wait."

"I'll polish up the plan some, give exact times of execution, units going where, over the next few days and resubmit it for your approval."

"Alright. What you've come up with is brilliant. I'll trust you with the final details."

A shadowy form came up to their table and interrupted them. Both military men jumped a little, reflexively, immediately settling when they saw it was the chief of police.

"Am I interrupting anything?" he asked.

"Not at all, Revu. Come, have a seat," Dan said, offering the man a chair. Neville rose and disappeared, coming back with a few cold bottles of Fiji Bitter, the chief's favorite. Twisting off the bottle top, he handed the chief the brew and put the other two unopened bottles in the bucket of ice.

"What can we do for you, Revu?" Dan asked.

"I've come to thank you for everything you've done."

"No need to thank us, Revu."

"I think it must be said, because these things have a habit of being forgotten after the deed."

"If you insist," MacDevitt said.

"My men, I tell you. I've never seen them so..."

"Motivated?" Dan offered.

"Yes. Your men have been earnest in the lessons, and my men have been quite eager to learn."

"Then all should work out," Dan said. "I do have to tell you this. About two weeks before D-Day, I'll be taking about a hundred of your men."

"Taking them where?"

"Revu, it's need to know. You'll have to trust me. In the next few weeks my men who've been teaching yours will assess all who've been undergoing training, and will give me a list of men I'll use for special jobs."

"I will trust you, Captain Kruger."

"Great." Dan grinned. "Now that that is settled, have another beer."

"Thank you. You both are too kind."

"Only doing what we think is right, Revu," MacDevitt said. "Remember, my wife is Korotongan. I plan on retiring here."

"I plan on building a tiki bar and about a dozen cottages along the shoreline, south of the palace. I'll bring money onto the island the right way, Aussie and Kiwi tourists!" Dan assured the older man. It was the first time he'd said it out loud, his idea that popped into his head one day. Though he still thought about the bungalow in Belize, and of Maria often, this was a wide open crapshoot for those first in to make a bundle of cash and help out the island's economy in a huge way.

"Oh, do you now?" The chief laughed at the idea.

"Always the capitalist, eh, Captain?"

"Nothing wrong with making a buck, as long as you don't oppress others in order to do so. Charity starts with the best capitalist. I start a business here, hire a bunch of locals from the start. Pay them a good wage, with decent hours."

"What everyone should do."

"But don't. Anyway, don't pay them slave wages, treat them like humans. A happy worker will pass on that same happiness to the customers, who'll do a few things. They'll be so happy with their stay at Dangerous Dan's Tiki Bar and Resort, they'll come back again, and tell all of their friends what a great time they had. Those people will come also, bringing in even more money. To me, and the locals in terms of wages and taxes. Everyone wins."

"If it's done right," MacDevitt emphasized.

"Maybe you should stay on here and work with the Minister for Tourism, Captain," Revu remarked.

"I'll keep that under advisement, gentlemen. Now I must call it a night. I have the early watch tomorrow morning, so I will now bid you both a fond *adieu*." Dan stood, pushed his chair aside, and with a slight two degrees list to starboard, he stumbled through the hotel, into the lobby and onto the street out front.

It was full dark and absolutely no traffic was on the road. Machinery noises could be heard from across the river at the docks, where two ore ships sat tied up, their waterlines never getting closer to the gunwales.

Two streetlights shone brightly, one in front of the hotel, and the other at the road intersection in front of the gas station on the far side of the river. Those they would have to take care of. Maybe take the power out for the whole town for a short while.

Meandering across the bridge, he peered down into the dark water of the Kota River. It was far too deep at this place to ford the tanks so the bridge had to stand, no matter what, if he wanted them at the palace gates.

He was constantly making mental notes in his head, like in the invisible margins to MacDevitt's plan. He imagined his new friend Yury saying *"Tovarisch! Simples!"*

It wasn't that simple, was it?

The one nut to crack he left for himself, the hardest one, was the radio station. Without that, everything else was lost. He couldn't fail.

He only had two choices, win, or die trying.

An unseen dog barked a few times as he passed the gas station as he closed in on the bougainvillea hedge that surrounded the presidential compound. When the two gate guards saw who it was, they snapped smartly to attention.

"Good evening, Captain Kruger."

"At ease, men. Good evening, Corporal. Is everything in order?"

"Yes, sir. It is mostly quiet, and the way it should be."

The private opened the huge wrought iron gates and let Dan pass through, closing and locking it behind him.

Alert but complacent, Dan thought about the guards at the gate. Something they'd need to consider in the final draft.

He looked up at the palace, and saw that only the president's bedroom suite had lights on. Ilikimi had the habit of staying up to all hours of the morning on any given day. Something else to chew over.

He made it all the way to his quarters and once inside, he stripped out of his uniform, tossing it into a clothes hamper by the bathroom. Wrapped in brown waxed paper, placed neatly at the foot of his bed were three more sets of clean, pressed, and starched uniforms fresh from the local laundry.

Standing in his underwear, he quickly unwrapped and hung them properly in the wardrobe so as not to get any fold creases. He then shucked the rest of his clothes, took a long hot shower, and climbed beneath clean, dry sheets.

As he was drifting off to sleep, he wondered how many times when he was still in the service of the United States of America was he afforded cleaned and pressed uniforms daily, maid service, crisp sheets on a comfortable bed, all with more pay a month than he'd ever been paid in a year, with nearly unlimited access to gourmet food and booze.

He wondered if he was not doing himself a huge disservice by plotting against his benefactor.

CHAPTER 11

"Are you fucking kidding me, Kruger?"

"What?" Dan asked, feigning innocence.

"What? *What?* All you have to say is '*what?*'"

"I told you when we talked a month ago that I was going to need assistance in getting certain items out of customs in Suva to—"

"Certain items?" Poindexter cut him off. "I said I would assist in getting some things through customs here, and over to the airport in Nadi. I did *not* agree to help you smuggle *a battalion's worth of arms and ammunition* into Korotonga!"

"I did remember asking you the same thing after you got shot down by Langley. Here's the stuff, the Fiji customs officials now all have new washers, dryers, refrigerators, stereos, and console TV's. High-end shit too. It wasn't cheap. You didn't have to do a goddamn thing. I did it for you. Now I need transport for these items to a hangar I've rented under a third party. We can get that done today, and no one at the embassy or back in DC will be the wiser."

Poindexter walked into the relative shade of the open shipping container, ran his fingers through his sweat-soaked hair, and let out a huge sigh. He looked right into Kruger's eyes, which never flinched, and shrugged.

"Hey, it's not like it's your OP. By this time tomorrow, we'll be completely out of Fiji with everything, and you'll never hear from us again," Dan lied smoothly.

"Okay, okay. Give me an hour or so to make a few phone calls."

"That's the spirit," Dan said, smiling broadly. He held the smile planted on his face until Poindexter was out of eyesight, and faced the three other men standing out of sight, though not out of earshot from the entire exchange.

Cleatus Snodgrass, one of his men from the protection detail, let out a long whistle. "Ooooh doggy! That gentleman is madder n' a one-nutted gator at a crawdaddy boil!" His thick Cajun accent made everyone laugh loud and hard.

"I'll say, Cap'n," José Jimenez agreed.

"What if he decided to fuck us, Captain?" Seamus Callaghan asked in a Northern Ireland accent that was as icy as the North Sea.

"He won't."

"The little fuck might, and if he does, we'll all be fucked," Callahan said, the last bit coming out as one word, *'wheelallbeefooked.'*"

"Oh ye of little faith."

"I'll cut his heart out," Seamus said as Poindexter rounded the side of the container.

"So what's the word?" Dan asked.

"I've got you transport. You're going to have to pay them, in cash, before they pull out of the lot."

"Now I wonder where they'd have gotten the idea to ask that?"

"I've got a few questions, by the way."

"Such as?"

"Where did you come across all of this? Shit, it's brand-fucking-new, Dan. All of it! This could not have come out of Afghanistan."

"You're right, none of it came out of Afghanistan," Dan agreed, less than forthcoming with further details.

"All this new Soviet equipment. How?"

"For me to know, Poindexter, and you to cry about. It took me weeks to get this shit, and cost me a lot more than it's worth to acquire and get here, out of my own pocket," Dan glibly lied. "I've also made a good contact in East Germany that you cannot have. End of story," Dan stated, leading Poindexter to think he got it from an East German source. Technically *that* was true. The source himself wasn't East German, he was Russian. Dan decided to leave that little tidbit out.

"The manifest says it was shipped out of Hamburg."

"Well then, there ya' go. That's about as much information as you are going to get."

"Fine. Shit, don't do anything completely nutty."

"Nutty, as in overthrowing the government of a legally recognized, sovereign nation?"

"Yeah, nutty like that."

"No worries, my man. I'm only providing the training and equipment, the locals are going to handle the pointy end of things."

"Are you sure?"

"Promise," Dan lied, and held out his right hand in a Boy Scout salute, "Scout's honor."

"Please, save me from it all. One last thing," the CIA man said as he was walking away, "is there anything else you like to ask of me? My left testicle, perhaps?"

"Maybe an entire US Marine Corps Amphibious Task Force sitting somewhere between Fiji and Korotonga in about three months?"

"Fat chance."

Dan grinned. "Thought I'd ask."

Poindexter stalked away, mumbling under his breath.

"You mean that?" Seamus asked.

"About the Amphibious Task Force?"

"Yeah."

"Goddamn right I was serious. Every little bit of an edge we can get, we're going to need and take advantage of."

"Dat boy oughta relax. He's so high strung he gonna stroke out," Cleatus said.

"Snodgrass, you should have seen him the day we met. Before our first meeting I thought I was going to have to do CPR on him."

"Imagine if he knew about the tanks," Jimenez pointed out with a smile.

"Oh, I'm sure blood would have shot out of his eyes."

"About those, Captain. Where are they?"

"Already on the LST, Seamus," Joey Sutcliff said, rounding the corner of the container, "We're ready to sail, Cap'n."

"Good to see you, Joey. So we're ready?"

"Yep. Ready to go. I've got about twenty men on the LST to assist in the reassembly."

"What about the BRDMs?"

"We'll have to come back for them. There's plenty of room on the deck for the containers once we get rid of the tanks."

"You mean we'll have to come all the way back to Suva?"

"No, my buddy, the skipper of the LST, tells me there's a cove about half-way between Lautoka and Varoka on the north end of the island, a little further than Nadi. He says the jungle is pretty thick right there, and the road is pretty well hidden. He gave me a map with exact details on how to get to this cove. Anyway, you go, get the tanks put together, I'll stay here. We'll get everything to Nadi and into the hangar you've rented there. After that I'll take the other containers with the BRDMs and the ammo and shit for the tanks, and get them to the cove."

"Where I'll come back and get them onto the LST. We won't need any cranes?"

"Nah, the skipper said that even at high tide, he'll be able to drive the ship right up onto the beach and open the front doors and ramp. Drive the fuckers in. There's not even any reef there to contend with."

"How did you work out getting the tanks off of the ship without going through customs?"

"That was the easy part. Turns out my buddy and the skipper of the cargo ship were together in the Portuguese navy. He satellite-phoned his buddy, and had the cargo ship heave-to about ten miles out to sea, where he sidled up with the LST, and with the exchange of some Johnny Walker Black, winched the behemoths from one deck to the other. I was told the exchange took less than ten minutes, with a smooth as glass sea that night."

"How's things on your end, Joey?" Dan asked, making sure everything was still going to plan.

"No worries on my end. Like I told you this morning on the flight over, I started to use the C119 every day on my flights, so as not to arouse suspicions. I used the excuse about a bad magneto in the C47 for good measure. So we get all the stuff you want airdropped to the hangar at Nadi. Me and the three musketeers over there," Joey said, pointing at Cleatus, Seamus and José, "we'll split the shipments into the drop containers and load them onto the plane. After dark, we fly to Korotonga and drop them onto pre-selected drop zones you boys will have marked for me with red lamps, like we did with the uniforms and incidentals."

"How about the night landings at Kotara?"

"I can land anything you want onto a postage stamp, blindfolded with a 100mph crosswind. Don't you worry about me, sonny!"

"I trust you," Dan said, stifling a laugh. He wasn't sure if Joey was kidding or not, but he looked kind of insulted right now.

"I know you do. It'll take about five to six nights to get everything dropped safely. I'm flying around the east side of the island and coming overland as to completely avoid any places where we might get spotted dropping the containers. The canopies aren't white, are they?"

"No, I specifically asked my supplier for green ones."

"Good, 'cause white canopies fucked us up on Guadalcanal back in '43, and I don't want a repeat."

"Then that's it," Dan said, more relieved that he'd care to admit. The closer they all got to D-Day, the more on edge all the men felt. Dan decided on the spot that as soon as this section of the mission was over, he'd throw a huge drunken party for them at the Grand Hotel in Kotara to let off some steam.

A few flatbed tractor trailers started to show up at this time, and Dan wandered over to them to insure they were his. When it was worked out who would do what, and Dan was thoroughly fleeced out of what little cash he had left, he departed the customs yard for where Joey told him the LST's skiff was waiting for him.

Secure in the knowledge that everything was in good hands here, he walked down the wharf and thought about his increasing times away from the presidential compound, and his taking some men with him each time. He'd have to come up with an alibi soon, or one day that little fuck Tiki would ask the wrong thing at the wrong time.

He found the skiff soon enough, and with the help of hand signals and a few words in pidgin, they were underway across the harbor to the anchored LST. Pulling alongside, Dan noticed that there were stairs lowered down the side, making it easy for him to come aboard, and once over the gunwale, he was shocked at the neatness and cleanliness of the ship.

If he didn't know better, he'd think this ship was still commissioned in the US Navy; it was that clean and shipshape. He was led to the bridge and introduced to the captain of the vessel, and discovered the ship was no longer the LST 369 in spite of the still bright white numerals painted on the side of the bow. Her name was now *O Célia* or *The Celia*, and was named after the captain's mother.

Dispensing with the small talk, the captain made a few sharp orders into the handset, and within minutes the anchor was weighed and they were underway. As soon as the island of Viti Levu slipped beneath the horizon to the south, Dan and the crew began pulling apart the wooden crates, and remembered the air-drop containers. As soon as the first plywood wall slabs fell away, there was a clamor of aluminum tubes and what looked a little like short torpedoes rolling around the deck.

Dan got a work party together and collected them all, placing them in a neat pile out of everyone's way at the aft portion of the main cargo deck. They got back to work on reassembling the T80s.

Yury had written out detailed instructions in English, Russian, and German, and Dan read them over twice to be sure he read them correctly. There were some slang terms in Russian for a few of the bits, but all in all, it took them less than five hours to re-install the four 125mm smoothbore main guns into the turrets, get each one fired up and everything tested.

Everything was working fine. He'd have to send Yury a thank-you note, and pondered whether he should send it to his laager back in East Berlin, or Lubyanka in Moscow?. Dan walked over to a wash basin and cleaned up, and headed to the bridge. Speaking with the captain, he found it would still be another ten hours before they reached Korotona at 0130 local time, with a new moon. The captain told him he wanted to get there, get the tanks unloaded, and be well below the horizon before the sun was up.

He dined with the captain that evening, allowing himself to be regaled by sea stories from the past, and he quite enjoyed himself. He wasn't altogether sure who had the better time, the old Portuguese sailor or himself. His money was on the old Portuguese sailor.

He excused himself from the table feeling quite stuffed, thanked his host profusely, and went to a small cabin he'd been afforded upon boarding. The plan, as it stood, was for Dan himself to take the T80s ashore by himself, and the LST would go back to Viti Levu in Fiji, collect the rest of the men, ammo, and BRDMs from the hidden cove, ferry those back to the island the following night, leaving Dan on Korotona alone for twenty-four hours.

He'd flown over the island numerous times with Joey, and noted it was unremarkable. Not very big at all, only a few feet at its highest point above sea level, and the only thing it looked like it was home to was hundreds of coconut palms and sea birds.

At exactly 0130 hours local time, the LST's prow slid to a silent stop on the soft, snow white beach of Korotona. The tide was out, and that left the hard, wet and packed sand for about fifty meters to the high tide mark, where there were another fifty meters to the tree line.

As the ramp came down, Dan stood on the deck and surveyed where he'd drive them. He frowned when he saw the wide strip of soft, dry sand above the high tide mark, and he called over to who he earlier found out was the chief of the deck hands.

He was confident enough with the 42.5 tons of tank on the wet sand, however, one slight mistake with the controls on the soft stuff and he'd have one hell of a problem getting the tank unstuck. With that in mind, he and the chief came up with a plan to use the plywood from the crates the tanks had been sheathed in, and lay down a hasty removable carpet of plywood over the dry sand up into the tree line.

That idea worked like a charm, and within fifteen minutes, Dan had all four tanks safely under cover inside the tree line on the island and parked, ammo and equipment offloaded, and plywood pulled up and placed under a few trees out of sight.

By the time the LST had vanished below the southeastern horizon, Dan had camouflage netting over and between the armored vehicles, and a hammock strung in between two of the tanks.

Kicking off his boots, he checked his luminous wristwatch in the dark. It was now almost 4AM. Grabbing a Fiji Bitter out of a cooler filled with ice the captain of the LST graciously loaned him, he climbed into the hammock.

Sipping on the beer, his mind spun for a few moments, checking and re-checking his many mental checklists. Once he was satisfied everything was going to plan, he finished his beer, got comfortable, and was quickly asleep.

≫≪

A little after noon, Dan took a large roll of masking tape, covering up the important signs in Russian, and writing over the tape with an indelible pen the English equivalent in all three of the crew stations.

Unlike Western tanks, Soviet tanks only had three crewmen—the driver, gunner, and tank commander—replacing the main gun loader with an automatic loader. This saved space and weight, giving the tank a lower overall profile, further cramping the already sparse, poorly designed, and user-unfriendly controls.

Ergonomics was a science they completely left out when they were designed. Dan squeezed himself out of the driver's compartment on the fourth tank. Looking at the time, he saw that it was getting close to 6PM. He readied a small fire pit in the sandy soil that he'd use to cook his supper once the sun went down.

The walls of the shallow pit would shield the fire from observers out at sea, and the darkness would hide any smoke. He placed a battery-operated infrared beacon on the beach, and after dusk he waded into the warm water to check the traps he'd built and placed earlier.

Finding a few fat crabs, he grinned and pulled them out of the water. After the crabs were cooked and a few more beers consumed, he doused the fire with seawater and headed back to the hammock for a few more hours' rest.

Startled awake hours later in the pitch black, he dropped to the ground and un-holstered his Browning High Power, peering out into the inky blackness of the night. It wasn't until a few moments had passed and his eyes adjusted to the darkness that he made out the darkened silhouette of the LST coming ashore.

He stood, reholstered the pistol, and walked toward the massive ship. He got to the foot of the ramp as it was settling on the packed wet sand below the high tide line.

"I take it everything is secured?" Joey asked.

"Yep, everything's settled here."

"We'll unload everything now, and get the shit cammo'ed, and take the ship back to the cove. I ditched a hire van there. We'll all go back to my place at the airport in Nadi, heading back to Kotara tomorrow afternoon."

"Sounds like a plan to me, Joey. Did you get the other drop containers?"

"Yeah," Joey said. He pulled Dan aside to let the BRDMs roll down the ramp unimpeded. "When we got the first shipment to the hangar, I thought there had to have been some mistake, and figured the rest were on the LST."

"If they hadn't been, we'd have been hard pressed getting the rest of the stuff onto Korotonga."

"That's true, skipper. Let's leave it to the hired muscle to get the rest of the gear onto the beach and hidden, and we'll mosey on up to the bridge and talk to the skipper some. He wants to talk to you about the early morning part of the D-Day landing with the tanks."

"Lead the way," Dan said, and the pair walked up the side of the front ramp, leaving the LST's crewmen to manhandle the wood cases of main gun rounds, coaxial and heavy machinegun rounds, and about fifty 55-gallon drums filled with diesel that Dan had purchased locally in Suva.

Once on the bridge, the captain beamed at Dan. "Captain Kruger," he said in thickly accented English, "your idea of landing those four tanks onto the beach in the main harbor in Kotara is not a wise one."

"Why's that, skipper?"

"The two breakwaters are too close together, and even at high tide, the current from the river is swift. LSTs like this one are designed to get in close to the beach, right onto it, so we have a very shallow draft. The eddies and currents that run through the mouth of the river would most likely see me founder on the breakwaters long before we got close enough to the shore to lower the ramp. To do it your way, I would need the assistance of tugboats like the ore ships."

"Not what I wanted to hear."

"I understand. I do have a remedy."

"Let's hear what you have in mind."

"Follow me," he said, motioning with his hand over to the chart table. When they all had gathered around, he turned on the overhead lamp that shone on an inset of a larger map, showing the beach along Kotara and the entire foreshore for about a mile north to south.

The Portuguese captain traced his finger along the shoreline of the big island, running north, stopping about halfway to the airport. "Right here is where I will take your tanks, armored cars, and men ashore."

Dan looked at it closely, and glanced back at the captain. "It looks like there's a reef in the way, skipper."

"Yes, yes, there's a reef there. At low tide with a new moon, I can nose my ship right onto the reef, lower the ramp, and your tanks, armored cars, and men will only have to wade about a hundred meters to shore, with water only a few centimeters deep. Not only that, the beach comes right up to the road there, so onto dry land, turn right, and head south again."

"I see. How is the sea floor between the reef and the beach, in the lagoon?"

"Wet sand and coral. Nothing too difficult to navigate."

"Thanks, skipper. I'll take that under advisement, and let you know well before D-Day."

"Not only that, Dan, it's far enough out of town as to not immediately draw attention," Joey said.

"Alright then, I'll do my own scouting of that area, and let you know before D-Day, skipper. I'll have to check the moon and tide charts to see if we'll have that low tide to work with the morning of D-Day. That's all I can promise right now."

Just then word came from down on the deck that they were secured from unloading on shore, and all hands were accounted for. The skipper made short work of getting back underway, and soon the big ship was nosing up to the beach into the hidden cove on Viti Levu on Fiji.

"What about these shipping containers, Dan?" Joey asked.

"I dunno. Got any spray paint?"

"I think so."

"Paint 'Take me, I'm free!' on all of them. Someone will put them to use."

"Good idea," Sutcliff nodded and vanished to find the paint.

Dan let out a yawn, and realized in spite of the sleep he got back on the deserted island, he was getting to the point of being dog-tired. After Joey found a brush and a can of yellow highway line paint in the back of the van and painted his signs, they all piled into the big vehicle for a quick trip to the airport in Nadi.

After a day's rest at Nadi, the crew loaded yet another delivery into the airdrop containers, loaded them into the

C119, and after securely locking the hangar with the rest of the gear and guns, Joey taxied the big twin-engine, twin-tailed cargo plane to the runway threshold, waiting for instructions from the tower.

After receiving the okay to take off, Joey slipped the brakes and throttled up to full power, and slowly began to roll down the macadam runway in the evening heat. The dense tropical air was thick with humidity, and the twin radial engines screamed as they clawed for altitude.

Once airborne, everyone except Joey nodded off, only to be awakened a few hours later in preparation for the airdrop.

Donning a pair of dark-tinted infrared goggles, Joey peered out into the blackness for the beacon. In spite of his age, he was still eagle-eyed and found the beacon before Dan, leveled off dangerously close between two peaks, and threw a switch on the control panel that illuminated an amber light on both sides of the rear bulkhead next to the jump doors that had already been opened in preparation for the drop.

As soon as the ground beacon disappeared beneath the nose of the big plane, Joey flipped another switch, turning that amber light to green, giving the men in the back exactly sixty seconds to get all twenty airdrop containers out of the door.

Joey made a few slight corrections in those sixty seconds with the throttles and control surfaces to adjust for the aircraft suddenly becoming two tons lighter. He did it by feel, and he was a professional, no doubt about that.

"So last night's drop went about the same?" Dan asked.

"Yeppers, no different. I reckon we've got four more nights like this, and we're done."

"I'll take your word for it."

"I don't know about you, Danny boy, but I'm getting a tad excited!" Joey said, facing Dan in the red light of the cockpit. He'd still not taken off the goggles, and his crooked teeth, wild hair, and evil grin made Joey look demonic, and for some ironic reason, settled Dan's nerves right down to a relaxing thrum that matched the beat of the radial engines purring away on the wing nacelles not ten feet away from him.

CHAPTER 12

It was two weeks before the Independence Day celebrations and in a rare spot where he had a little down time, Dan was sitting propped up in bed in his quarters at the palace, smoking cigarettes, drinking beer, and reading Stephen King's *The Stand* for the third time.

He had managed to get the roster working to the point where at least two of his men were off for two days, giving them time to rotate around training the island's police in infantry tactics, rifle marksmanship with the new weapons, and getting handfuls of men over to Korotona under the cover of darkness to train on the BRDMs and the tanks, all without being found out.

Things were running smoothly, so he used this time for a little relaxation. He found if he got too involved, he tended to micromanage, and since he hated doing that, he decided to let the men take care of things. When someone rapped on his outside door frame, he merely looked up from his book and called, "Come."

Neville poked his head in. "Not disturbing anything, sir?"

Dan sat up and closed his book using a Fijian $2 note as a bookmark. "Not at all, come on in. Beer's in the fridge."

Neville walked in, followed by Ernst Bauer. Shutting the door behind him, MacDevitt went to the fridge, pulled out two bottles of Miller High Life, handed one to Ernst, pulled a chair around to face the bed, and sat down.

"What's the skinny?"

"We've got problems, Cap'n," MacDevitt stated.

Dan quickly sat up in bed, book totally forgotten, "What problems, Sar' Major?"

"I'll let the sergeant tell you himself."

"Well, sir," Ernst said, "I notice little things, and things aren't sitting right with me. A week ago, Tiki ordered the colonel-general in charge of the army to start some patrols in the jungle between here, the radio station, and the mine, because of, I quote, 'increased marauder activity.' He's doubled the garrison here. Showed up about an hour ago, and it's got a lot of new faces, and those faces are telling me they know."

"They know what, our plans?"

"I believe so, sir."

"Is this a hunch, or do you have something more solid?"

"Why else double the garrison here, Dan?" MacDevitt asked.

"True. It's still a little thin though."

"Sir, they've reinforced the radio station with another company of infantry, and the Jap tank. They've also built a few bunkers out of palm logs outside of the building, sandbagged the generator, and felled trees on the road leading up to the mountain's summit."

"That's not so thin. Anything else?"

"I'm not sure if you've heard them this morning or not, but there's now a manned Matilida tank at the front gate, and two Shermans bracketing the north side of the bridge."

"They know," Dan whispered.

"Aye, they bloody well know. And we've got a rat in our midst," MacDevitt spat.

"That we do, Nev. Who?"

"Whoever it is either hasn't told them the whole plan, or doesn't know the whole plan, only the outline."

"Aye, Ernst, do you have any ideas?"

"I do, although I'm a little hesitant to say..."

"Why?" MacDevitt demanded.

"Because he's a close friend of the captain's from Vietnam."

"Nguyen? I wouldn't say he's a close friend, though we did serve together."

"May I be frank, sir?"

"*Ja*. Frank and open," Ernst said, sounding relieved.

"Sir, before you came here, he ran our clan with an iron fist. Maxime tried, and was many times successful in reining him in. Then when you came, things changed with him. He goes about the motions, never does any work."

"So he's a Blue Falcon. Being a buddy fucker and escalating to a traitor are two different things."

"There's more, Captain. I've seen him four times now enter the palace after dark when he's supposed to be on his rounds, exiting some time later with Tiki."

"Aye, that would be the deciding vote, Dan. Besides, there is one more way to look at it. He and Lukas Verheyen are the only two men in the unit that don't know the entire plan, only the part they're directly connected to."

"Why not Lukas?" Dan asked.

"He told me he only wanted to know his part, not the big picture in case he was captured. He wouldn't be able to tell them what he didn't know."

"What about Nguyen?"

"Well, he was never around all that much."

"Goldbricking. If he was goldbricking though, why now go to the president or Tiki to rat us out?"

"Perhaps he's securing his safety. You know exactly what can and will happen if Ilikimi arrests us for an attempted coup."

"Yeah. We're violating two dozen international laws and breaking a few treaties in there too. We can be tried as spies and hanged, and not a government on Earth will lift a finger to help us."

"So the little bastard is ratting us out and making it safe for him when it's all over?" Ernst asked.

"Looks that way," Dan said.

"That skinny little fuck!" Ernst shouted. "I will kill the *untermench* myself!"

"No, no. That's not going to help us a bit. Leave it to me, I will handle it."

"*Ja*, yes, I apologize for letting my emotions get the better of me."

"No worries, Ernst. Go and get some rest." Ernst nodded and let himself out of Dan's room.

"So what do you think?" Dan asked Neville when Ernst was out of earshot.

"I think we've got to rethink our plans, Dan."

"I concur. First thing first. Get word to the men north of here this afternoon. Cease all firearms training and locate a new place to shoot. Scrub the old place clean. I don't want a trace of us ever being there to be found, and I mean it. Not even a half-whiff of a monkey fart."

"Aye."

"I want to pull two mortars from the raids on the barracks and augment them into the attack on the radio station. Figure out which police squad will only get one mortar for their mission. We've only eight mortars. With the reinforcement of the radio station, we're gonna need two of those tubes."

"Anything more, Captain?"

Dan lit a Marlboro, blowing out a cloud of blue smoke. "Yeah. We originally planned for a dawn attack on the morning of Independence Day. As I recall, last year's celebrations were quite the drunken affair..."

"Aye, I see where you're going now."

"How about changing D-Day until the day after Independence Day, and Zero hour around 0300, not 0600?"

"All parties will be hungover or still fairly well still drunk. I like the idea more and more, sir."

"Also, it works out better for the LST and the armor. The tides won't be perfect, but they'll be a whole lot more favorable the morning after Independence Day."

"Got it. What about the issue with Nguyen?"

"Leave that with me, Neville. And not a word on the changes in the plan until I have handled that situation."

"No worries, Dan.

"Anything else?"

"I have your mess dress jacket and tie for our dinner tonight with the major. I played hell getting all of your medals in miniature."

"Thanks for reminding me. I've been looking forward to this like I've been secretly longing for a root canal."

"Shit, you've been wanting to recce his place for the heavy mortars now for a while. Here's your chance."

"I know, I know. I hate these formal things, especially when they're irrelevant."

"I'll drop the jacket off in an hour, Dan."

"Yeah, okay. If you see Callaghan, tell him to come see me, okay?"

"No problem, Captain," MacDevitt said, closing the door behind him, leaving Dan alone with his thoughts.

He swept his room nightly for 'bugs' and had never found any, so he wasn't worried about eavesdropping electronically, although he wished he could have gotten a bug into the president's office.

At a knock on his door, he opened it to be greeted by Seamus Callaghan's smiling face.

"Sar' Major says you were lookin' for me?"

"Yeah, come in," Dan said, ushering him into the room. "I'll make it short and sweet, Seamus. I need to ask you if you can put something together for me for tonight?"

"Sure 'ting, Cap," Seamus said, and when Dan told him what he needed, the smile vanished and his eyes grew as wide as saucers.

"Can you do it?"

"Yeah, I can do it. Why?"

"You don't need to know now," Dan whispered.

"When would ye be needin' it by tonight?"

Dan checked the roster, ran his finger down the list until he found the name, and ran his finger along until he stopped on that day's date. After doing a little mental calculation in his head, he looked back at Callaghan and replied, "Midnight. Bring it here to my room."

"Alright then. Let me get to me artistry."

Alone again, Dan drank another beer, showered, and shaved in preparation for tonight's soiree.

Once on his way up the long drive to the major's house at the top of the hill, he did think that both he and MacDevitt looked good in their mess-dress formal attire. MacDevitt pulled the Land Rover up in front of the huge colonial house, by the steps to the wide covered veranda. An East Indian man of undetermined age scurried out of the shade, dressed completely in white *mundu*.

The manservant bowed, and led both soldiers up the stairs, across the veranda, and into the huge house, down a long carpeted corridor to a library.

"Please help yourselves to refreshments, the major will be along shortly," the manservant stated with a bow, and disappeared out a side door.

The pair looked at each other and shrugged. MacDevitt went to the wet bar first.

"At least the blighter has good booze," he said, pouring himself three fingers of triple malt Scotch. "For you captain?"

"If there's Bombay Gin, I'll take that with tonic and a slice of lime."

"One Bombay gin and tonic on the way."

"Some house, eh? It's like a museum," Dan remarked.

"Aye. Homage to several centuries of glorious defeat. Did you take a look at the paintings in the hallway?"

"I did, however, I'm not familiar with that much British military history."

"Every last one of those paintings out there is of battles the British army lost."

Dan walked to a formal fireplace with mantel and looked up at an oil portrait of a British officer from a different century. "I wonder who this guy is?"

"That, Captain, is Brigadier Percy Smithe-Woodrising, my grandfather."

Dan turned to see the major by the wet bar fixing himself a beverage. Impeccably dressed in his uniform, bearing medals that were unfamiliar to Dan, all from the British Army, were gleaming from his chest.

A gold monocle rounded out the image, and Dan almost laughed out loud. He quickly caught himself and sidled up to MacDevitt. "You could have warned me that he was a dead ringer for Terry-Thomas..." Dan whispered.

Dan was one hundred percent correct; from the mustache to the gap between his front teeth, the major was a dead ringer for the British comedian, Terry-Thomas.

Dan shook the man's hand firmly. "Captain Daniel Kruger, United States Army, Retired."

"It's a pleasure to finally meet you, Captain. I understand you've been quite busy with President Ilikimi's protection detail."

"That is true, Major."

"Well now, don't let all your work consume you. That's what your junior grade officers and other ranks are for," the major replied, completely indifferent to MacDevitt, a sergeant major.

"I'll try not to be a stranger, Major."

Another manservant entered, dressed similarly to the first one, and bade them all into the dining room. The table was set for three, and could easily have seated two dozen. Everything about the house screamed of the upper crust of

England, and Dan wondered if making it so much like home only accentuated how far from home he was.

Dinner was traditional roast beef, Yorkshire pudding, and roasted Brussels sprouts, and Dan complimented the chef. It truly was delicious, and Dan thought that perhaps he should chat up the major more often, if for anything, a home-cooked meal.

After dessert of blackberry and apple crumble, the major suggested after dinner cocktails and a smoke on the veranda, and Dan used the fantastic view and sunset as an excuse to roam freely in the garden.

Once outside, his fourth gin and tonic in his hand, Dan complimented the major on the view.

"I always figured you had a nice view out here, Major, though never in my wildest ideas did I think you had *this* sort of view. It's stunning."

"I'm glad you like it, Captain. My family has over one hundred acres on top of the mountain here. We used to have more, so much more, land. That's all gone now."

"Did you grow up here?"

"Oh heavens no, Captain. I was sent back to England for my schooling. My parents stayed on, and it wasn't until after the Great War I was able to come back."

"Then to Singapore?"

"Yes, to that sordid little affair. If we'd had only a little more time, you know? That's all we needed."

"True," Dan said. What he really wanted to say was *No! You fuckers needed a goddamn spine! The Japanese came overland on goddamn bicycles, and you lot gave up!* He held his tongue in check; he needed to keep on this man's good side for now.

"I see there's an old coastal battery over there," Dan said, changing the subject before he said something to inflame the major. He could see MacDevitt already was having a time keeping his thoughts in check.

"Ah yes. Completely overgrown now, though it's still intact. Fourteen-inch guns, two of them. There's neither a shell nor powder in the magazines, and one would need a dozen men with machetes to uncover it."

"I love exploring places like that. I also understand there's miles and miles of Japanese tunnels throughout the island."

"My days of exploring are over, Captain. I've still got some damned poxy foreign lead in my gammy leg. Don't get around much anymore."

"That's a shame," Dan stated sadly. "Neville, have you seen the view from here?"

"I don't believe I have, Captain." MacDevitt replied, and moved over to stand close to Dan.

Dan pointed out to the setting sun and whispered, "I want one mortar tube there, and the other one on the far side of the patio. We'll be able to lob them straight down with very little charge."

"Agreed."

"Major, could I trouble you for another drink?" Dan asked, turning away from MacDevitt, who was making notes in a notepad.

"Of course!"

The three soldiers made small talk as the major regaled them from one improbable war story to another while an Indian manservant fixed cocktail after cocktail, and it was close to 11PM when Dan begged off another drink.

The major, quite satisfied he'd put on a great party, walked them to the front door and bade them a good night. His last words were a welcome back anytime, that Dan, a little drunk at this point, agreed to readily.

When MacDevitt slid behind the wheel of the Land Rover, Dan asked, "Are you alright to drive?"

"Fuck no, laddie. But I'm sure as fuck not lettin' you drive!"

MacDevitt started the engine and raced down the twisting, steep driveway in the pitch black night.

"Cap'n, you've got to die of something, might as well die spectacularly!"

A somber wave washed over Dan. "I can't. I still have one more chore I need to take care of..."

"Och, 'tis a shame, ruining a good drunk like that, especially on the major's quid."

Dan stared off into the jungle in the night. Neither man said anything until they had parked by their quarters inside the palace compound.

"What are you going to do?"

"Don't worry about that," Dan whispered. "All hell is going to break loose in less than an hour so act completely surprised."

"Wilco, Captain."

Dan left MacDevitt and stepped into the darkness to his room. Stripping down to his underwear, he looked at his watch, saw that it was midnight.

He sat in the darkness until a quiet knock at the door came.

"Come," he said, and walked towards the door. In the darkness, he saw the door open, and a sliver of light slashed out as Dan reached for and found purchase on Callaghan's wrist.

"Oi! Fook, Cap'n, you scared the fooking shit outta me!" he shouted as he was dragged into the darkened room.

"Keep your fucking voice down!" Dan hissed. "Were you able to make it?"

"Yeah, yeah, I made it."

"Good," Dan said, and turned on the light.

"Cheesus, Cap'n! Put some fookin' clothes on willya?"

"Don't worry about that, show me what you've got."

"It ain't pretty, but these things are rarely made for a fashion statement," Callaghan said. He handed over a green canvas package that Dan took and opened, holding it at eye level, turning it this way and that.

"It's got fifteen kilos of Semtex. I used some of the stash you got from the Russians. More than enough to do the trick."

"Thanks. Now get the fuck out of here, and be really, really surprised at what's about to happen."

"Cap'n, is that thing going to go boom?"

"Christ, I hope not."

"I'll take me leave then," Callaghan said, and with a flash, he was out the door.

Dan looked again at the bomber's vest he'd ask Callaghan to make for him, shuddered, and wondered why would anyone ever want to blow themselves up.

He remembered one time, a long time ago in Vietnam, he was forced to call in artillery on his own emplacement because his entire firebase had been overrun with Viet Cong. However, strapping explosives to your body and walking into a crowded room, building, or marketplace was a completely different animal.

Although the Viet Cong weren't averse to doing it, the fanatical reveled in it, especially the religious nuts.

"Seventy-two virgins my ass," Dan muttered. "Who the fuck wants that?" He shook his head at the insanity of it all, picked up the suicide vest, turned off the lights, and slid silently out onto his rear deck.

CHAPTER 13

Dan dropped down to the ground from his rear deck and crouched, listening to see if anyone heard his movements. Hearing nothing save some errant tree frogs, he crept along the rear wall of the guards' barracks to the north end and peered around the corner.

In the dim light of a last quarter moon, the long stretch of lawn between his position and the palace was visible. Seeing no one moving, he squatted down with his back against the wall and waited.

Shortly thereafter, Nguyen San and Hugh Martin come into view from the north. San motioned for Hugh, an Aussie, to head off in the direction of due west.

The Aussie headed off westward, taking him between the guards' quarters and the palace. Nguyen stood still and waited until Hugh was out of sight, then made a move to head around to the rear entrance to the palace.

It was now or never. Crouching low, Dan made a mad sprint. He hit Nguyen with his left forearm, dropped the explosives vest, and reached quickly between the man's legs and grabbed his belt buckle, throwing the Vietnamese man off balance and face first onto the grass.

Nguyen fought back nonetheless, and tried to kick at Dan, who was now sitting on his back. Nguyen San screamed and, still holding onto his Sterling sub machine gun, let loose a quick burst to send out the alarm.

The Vietnamese man was quick, and somehow was able to toss Dan aside and unsheath a commando knife from his duty belt. Swinging the blade wildly, he caught Dan in the right arm. Hugh had shown back up to render assistance, brought by the sound of the machine gun fire.

He was caught in the throat by Nguyen's razor sharp and pointy blade, and a spray of thick, bright red arterial blood gushed out of the wound and bathed all three.

Hugh died a quick, loud, and messy death. Loud air-raid type sirens were now blaring, lights were coming on all over the compound, and civilian bodyguards and soldiers alike were rushing to the bloody scene between the barracks and palace.

Dan took his right hand, balled it into a ham-sized fist and rapidly pummeled Nguyen San's face as hard as he could, as fast as he could. With each blow, his victim's face got softer and softer, Dan's blows becoming more and more savage. For a brief moment, Dan thought he could see the man who this used to be in the eyes he stared at with every blow. In the end, however, he stopped when he saw the last light of life leave the supine form on the ground.

Dan glanced around, and seeing his chances quickly fading, grabbed the explosives vest and threw it on the now very dead Vietnamese man. Dan was shaking violently from the adrenaline crash and was aware of others rushing up and surrounding him.

"Quick! Get a medic! Hugh's hurt!" Dan shouted.

"Too late for him, laddie!" MacDevitt replied, clad also in his boxer shorts, holding a Browning 9mm pistol at the ready. "You there! Secure this perimeter and make sure the bleedin' president is okay!" Dan stood and looked around the mayhem he'd committed, and shook his head. "Sar' Major!"

"Sir!"

"Get everyone in full gear and have them stand-to in ten minutes. I want a perimeter of one hundred meters, and I want to know for certain the president is safe, got it?"

"Got it, Cap'n!" MacDevitt loudly assented. "You heard the man, stop yer' lollygagging and I want a full equipment stand-to in less than ten minutes!"

Those men that were close by disappeared in a flash and lights flashed on in the rooms Dan and his men shared. Several Korotongan soldiers were milling around, not sure what to do. MacDevitt let it be made crystal clear he still wanted a one hundred meter perimeter, thank you very much.

"What is going on here?" Tiki's unmistakable nasal voice demanded loudly.

"Sir," Dan said, coming to attention. He was quite the sight, clad only in his boxer shorts, covered from head to toe in blood. "I'm not sure what has happened completely. Apparently Nguyen San was wearing an explosives laden vest and was heading to the palace for some reason. I heard Pvt. Hugh Martin shout out. As you were probably aware, myself and the sar' major had a dinner engagement with the major on the hill this evening, and had only just gotten back to the barracks."

"And what?" demanded a furious Tiki.

"Well sir, I was out on the back deck having my last smoke of the evening when I saw San followed by Hugh rush around this side of the palace. It looked to me as if Hugh was chasing San. Anyway, that's when I heard the gunfire and Hugh's shouts for help. I dropped down from by balcony, ran here, and saw Hugh trying to stop San from going any farther. When I attempted to break up the fight, San was far too quick, and he was able to get a knife out and hit Pvt. Martin in the throat. It was then I saw in the moonlight the suicide vest." Dan stepped back a little and pointed down at the body of the very dead Nguyen San.

"Suicide vest?" Tiki said loudly, his voice jumping a few octaves.

"Yeah. Looks like about fifteen kilos of plastic explosives."

"W-w-what do you think he was doing?" Tiki asked, shaking like a leaf.

"I don't know. Like I said, from what I can gather, he was heading to the palace when his partner, Hugh, got an idea of what he was doing, and tried to stop him. Looks like it got him killed, for what that's worth."

"I see that. I will make sure his next of kin gets a handsome bonus."

"A lot of good that'll do him. I'm pretty sure he'd have much rather seen the sunrise tomorrow."

"I'm sure, Captain Kruger."

"If you'd like, I'll do what investigation I can, and report back to you as soon as possible."

"Could you, Captain? I'd much rather not have the chief of police involved."

"I'll keep it internal, Tiki."

"I'm sure you'll have the utmost discretion, Captain."

"My men and the soldiers here have everything under control. Go ahead and go back to bed," Dan said, knowing damn well the diminutive man standing before him will not be able to get back to sleep tonight. The sheer volume of blood at the macabre scene alone would have even some of the most jaded homicide cops shaken.

Two Korotongan soldiers were standing by, ready to do whatever they were told.

"You two men get some tarpaulins and cover these bodies. I'm going up to my room to have a shower and get some clothes on," Dan ordered and left the soldiers to go to his room.

He was met halfway down the stairs by MacDevitt and a few other men from the security detail.

"What now, Cap'n?"

"I've got a huge seed of doubt planted in Tiki's head right now. Some soldiers are fetching some tarps up, and going to cover the bodies. Get every light in the compound lit, and get the men to team up with the Korotongan soldiers and make a perimeter. And remember," Dan hissed out a final order, "we're all one big, gigantic family, happy to be helping out, blah, blah, blah."

"Copy you five by five, Cap'n. We're so close I'm about to invite them all to fuck my sister," Cletus Snodgrass said.

"Once you've got that handled, grab Maxime Chauvet and Ernst Bauer and the three of you meet me in Nguyen San's room."

"Wilco, Cap'n," MacDevitt said, and headed down to the scene.

Dan went to his room, and went directly to the shower to scrub all the blood off his body.

He dried off and donned a fresh uniform, then went to San's room, where he easily broke in. Once inside, he methodically went through all of his personal papers.

He could read Vietnamese, and it embarrassed him to be reading such personal exchanges between San and his wife. He did serve with the man almost fifteen years ago, though to be honest with himself, he hardly knew the man at all.

Nothing appeared awry, and he was ready to give up when he found the letter hidden under his mattress. Along with the letter, a photo showed a frightened Asian woman, no doubt San's wife, teary-eyed and holding a newspaper dated a week ago Friday.

Dan read the letter twice, and became angry.

Why the fuck didn't he come to me?

Dan was still steaming when MacDevitt, Chauvet, and Bauer entered the room.

He gathered them around the table and sent Ernst to get two more chairs. While they waited for his return, Dan put the kettle on the range to make instant coffee. It was going to be a long night.

Dan passed around the letter he'd found along with the photo. He translated loosely what was said, and when that was done, lit a Marlboro and tossed his lighter onto the middle of the table as if to add an exclamation point.

"I wish he'd have come to one of us," MacDevitt said.

"Same thing I thought," Dan said. "But this will help us."

"How so, *Capitaine*?" Maxime asked.

"How much would you wager anyone here besides me on this island can read and speak Vietnamese?"

"None."

"Exactly. So who's saying this letter doesn't say 'blow up Ilikimi or you'll never see your wife and family again' not 'send us five million US dollars or you'll never see your wife and family again?' I mean, shit. It's got to work for us," Dan said in exasperation.

"You know, it might work," Ernst Bauer said.

"I just wish he'd not have taken Hugh with him," MacDevitt said.

"I agree. Too late now to lament over that though."

"Am I to gather he was approached by people smugglers to get his wife and family out of Vietnam?" Ernst asked.

"Yeah, he did tell me that much when I first got here. He told me that was the reason he was here, making enough money to pay off the smugglers to get them all to the Philippines."

"So if it wasn't anything he was hiding, why all the subterfuge?" MacDevitt asked.

"I'm reckoning he was approached by the people smugglers, and they demanded more and more money."

"Instead of coming to one of us," MacDevitt said, "he went to his employer and asked 'how much would this information be worth to you' and Tiki ate it up."

"Yeah. He went to Tiki, knew he needed a huge chunk of serious coinage, and gave up our plans."

"Not all of them."

"True, not nearly all of them," Dan agreed.

"Enough to fuck them up," Ernst spat.

"This can be repaired, and we still might come out of this smelling of roses."

"How so?"

"C'mon, haven't you been listening?"

"Assume I'm from Missouri," MacDevitt said coolly and Dan laughed until tears came to his eyes. When his laughter subsided, he took a sip of his now tepid coffee and spelled it out for them.

He held up the letter in scrawled Vietnamese. "Let's say that this says, 'we know who you work for. Do exactly as I say and you'll get to see your wife and children again. Get close to President Ilikimi by whatever means available, and once close,' yadda yadda yadda."

"The one thing that's a huge stickler for me, *Capitaine*—and correct me if I'm wrong—if he expects to see his family again, he wouldn't be blowing himself up, now would he?" Maxime said flatly, like a door slamming.

"Okay, I didn't think that one as far out as I should have. That's why I have you all here, to brainstorm."

"Now wait a moment," MacDevitt said, "he might, if his hand was forced."

"What do you mean?" Dan asked.

"Several years ago, in another Third World shithole I'm all too familiar with, the local warlords gave a handful of suicide bombers exactly this sort of ultimatum. Blow yourselves up to further the cause, or your entire family will suffer."

"No one can be that cruel," Ernst protested.

When everyone grew silent, Dan's eyes went from one to another seated at the dead man's table, trying to look into each and every one's soul.

"Alright, are we in agreement?"

"I guess I'll speak for everyone, Dan," MacDevitt said.

"One thing. I'm not digging the fact that we're sullying a man's reputation in order to further our means."

"I do not like it myself, *Capitaine*," Maxime said.

"What do we do to rectify it?" Dan asked. "I'm fucking serious. This pulls us out of one jam and lets us get back to our main goal. But really, I'm having a hard time with this in my head."

"I hear you, Dan."

"Do you, Neville?" Dan picked up the black and white photo of what was once a stunningly beautiful Vietnamese woman and tossed it to MacDevitt. "She likely has no idea her husband is dead. She's probably not seen him since the fall of Saigon twelve goddamn years ago! All she has is the promise that he made to her and their children that he'd come back for them."

"It is fucked, Dan."

"Yeah, it is Neville. So many years, so many fucked up things we've done. When does it all become right?" Dan said wistfully.

"How about right now?"

"Okay, lay that one out on me, because I'm at a fucking loss. He's laying out there in the grass with a face that I beat with these hands," he held them up for emphasis, "so badly I don't even think his fucking mother would recognize him."

"Dan, how did you pay for all of the gear we're getting? The tanks, the BRDMs, the rifles, machine guns, grenades, and the mortars?"

None of the men knew that he had broken into Ilikimi's private Swiss bank account. Nor did they know that he had financed this whole dirty little war out of that account. What hit Dan all of a sudden, like a lightning bolt, was the fact that every time he'd checked since he'd come back from West Germany, the account grew and grew, and that 30 million dollars that in one day had been transferred, had been obliterated by the mass of new money.

"I see what you're saying. I was hoping to talk to Taito Yasi about that first."

"I'm pretty goddamn sure he'll be okay with whatever you decide, Dan."

"What are you two going on about?" Maxime asked, perplexed.

"What Neville means, Maxime," Dan said, "is that all of the finances that have paid for all of the equipment we've been able to amass came right out of Ilikimi's private Swiss bank account."

Both Maxime and Ernst stared at Dan wide eyed, mouths agape, until the silence was broken by MacDevitt. "Alright, close yer goddamn mouths or you'll start catching blowflies."

"How much is in there?" Ernst asked.

"Well over eight digits right now."

"Eight digits... that's over a *billion* dollars!"

"Yeah, it's not ours. It's belongs to the people of Korotonga. Yeah, I bought all the stuff—guns, ammo, tanks—with that money, those things are staying here to revitalize the nation's new army once we go about it. I didn't use a cent of that money to line my pockets."

"He means it, gentlemen," MacDevitt stated with the finality of a casket slamming shut.

"We are mercenaries. Granted, we could split now and be filthy rich. And believe me, I was tempted. We've got how many people enslaved up at the mine, with more heading there every day, all to line the pockets of one asshole? Sure, I want to be rich one day, but not at the expense of another. We'll need to talk to Yasi about setting up a trust fund for Nguyen San's family, and also a decent one for Hugh's next of kin. He deserves as much also."

"It seems only right, considering we're about to drag his name through the mud."

"If we do it right," Dan said, "that fable will die with everyone over at the palace."

"Alright, that's done and dusted," MacDevitt said. "I need Maxime and Ernst here to go down and take care of those bodies. In this heat they're going to puff up and start to stink quickly."

"Consider it done," Ernst said, standing, followed by Maxime.

Dan checked his watch and saw that it was 5AM. "Neville, I know it's sort of unfair since you've been up as long as I have, and you've dealt with the major with me, but I'm pulling rank and getting some sleep."

"No worries, laddie. I'll make sure that the bodies are taken care of, get a few hours' shuteye meself, then come and get you for your report you'll have to give to Ilikimi and Tiki."

"Not before 10 AM."

"No worries, Dan."

"Thanks."

"Ah fuck, have ye ever seen such a clusterfuck?"

"Vietnam was one giant clusterfuck, Neville."

"Then I'm glad I never went."

"Count your blessings."

CHAPTER 14

"Captain Kruger, you're telling me that Lieutenant Nguyen San was being forced into getting close to the president in order to kill him?"

"That appears to be the case, Tiki," Dan said. "Says it all right there in these letters I've found."

"Disturbing."

"That it is. I'm sorry it came this close. I'd have handled it much differently if I'd known sooner. Let me ask you something, Tiki. Did he come to you recently with some tales?"

"Eh, no, not that I know of," Tiki said, and Dan knew he was lying.

"I figured he was fabricating tales to get close to the president. Either way, I wish I'd have been able to rectify this. I mean, he was one of my men."

"Hopefully this whole sordid affair is finished."

"I hope so too, Tiki. I think it's about finished up now."

"Yes, yes it is. I do have one question, Captain. Who exactly was blackmailing Nguyen San?"

"That I'm clueless about. I've gone over all of the letters, and the best I figure the extortion started about six months ago. He never saved any of the envelopes, so I couldn't see a postmark to give me some clue as to who would want to harm the president."

"It is a sad state of affairs. Captain Kruger, you saw the man with the explosives vest on, and could have been blown up yourself. You beat the man with your fists. Quit impressive in itself."

"Doing the job, Tiki. I was hired to protect the president, and I had no other weapons."

"It was still impressive. That will be all, Captain."

"I'm sure you have to make your report to the president, so I'll leave you to it."

"Thank you, Captain. Good day."

"Are the celebrations still set for next week?" Dan asked.

"Yes, nothing has changed as of yet."

"Great. I love a good parade. I'm looking forward to it."

"Good, good," Tiki said quietly and Dan took that as a cue and left. He exited the rear doors of the palace, rounded the corner where the grass was stiff and red with blood, and he remembered, right then and there, so vividly, his first day at the bayonet training range and Ft. Benning Georgia twenty years before...

The drill sergeant shouted out, "What is the spirit of the bayonet?"

The whole company shouted back, "To kill!"

"How does the green, green grass grow?" the drill sergeant asked a fired-up company.

"With blood! Red, red blood!"

"Where does that blood come from?"

"It comes from my enemies, from the tip of my bayonet!"

"And how does the green grass grow?"

"The blood of my enemies!"

"How does it flow?"

"From my bayonet!"

"What's the bayonet for?"

"To kill! To Kill! To Kill!"

It was a great motivator for a bunch of 18 year olds. Now, nearing 40, and seeing the blood was brought by his own fists was one great kick in the nuts.

Dan hopped behind the wheel of the detail's Land Rover and rolled out. Slowing for the soldiers at the front gate, he looked at his bruised and battered knuckles where they rested at twelve o'clock on the steering wheel.

So deep was his concentration that he didn't notice the corporal wave him through the first time, and it wasn't until the Korotongan soldier slapped his hand on the hood that Dan jumped into action.

"Are you okay, Cap'n?" the corporal asked.

"Yeah, thanks for asking, just a lot on my mind."

"Have a nice day, sir."

"You do the same." Dan released the clutch and sped out of the palace compound, heading north. He crossed the bridge, passed the two tanks, and made a quick left, pulling up to a stop at the Grand Hotel.

As he breezed through the lobby, he caught sight of Ernst, hastily buttoning his fly, coming out of the men's room.

"Ernst!"

"*Ja*, Captain?"

"Have you seen the sar' major?"

"*Ja*, he's out on the back veranda with Maxime," said the large German man.

"Meet us out there once you've got yourself put back together," Dan said, and continued to walk through the bar, nodded at the day bar staff, and went out onto the back deck, straight over to the far table at the very back.

Both Maxime and MacDevitt stood when Dan approached the table, and Dan waved at them to sit down. "At ease," he said, snatching a cold Miller High Life out of an ice-filled bucket sitting in the middle of the table. He twisted off the cap, flipped it like a quarter at MacDevitt, and plopped heavily onto the closest empty chair.

"We back on track, laddie?"

"Yeah, he bought it, the whole kit and caboodle," Dan replied, taking a long pull off the bottle of beer. "I would like to have seen the look on his face, *mon ami*," Maxime said with a little too much glee.

Dan snorted. "You could see the color drain out of him. As black as he is, he paled."

"He's never met anyone like you," MacDevitt said, sipping on a gin and tonic.

"True. Enough of that," Dan said. "Maxime, get hold of Revu Karalaini. Tell him we'll start tonight on sending the men over to Korotona."

"So everything's a go?" Ernst said, pulling up a chair and sitting down.

"D-day is now +14 days, gentlemen. We'll get the men over to Korotona and get them trained up on the T80s and the BRDMs. I hope two weeks is enough time."

"It'll have to be," MacDevitt stated.

"We'll sit tight here, and see if Ilikimi feels relaxed enough to stand down those extra men at the palace and get rid of those fucking tanks," Ernst muttered.

"Exactly," Dan said. "Even if he doesn't though, we can handle them."

"I'd rather not. Least amount of bloodshed, the better," MacDevitt stated.

"Alright then. Don't go out on a limb, okay?" Dan called for the bartender to bring another 'Bucket O' Beer' as he'd started calling them, and when the fresh bucket arrived, he popped the top and downed yet another one.

"Here's another question that's been nagging me. Where the hell are the other three Shermans, two Churchills, and one Matilda tank?"

"No one seems to know," Maxime answered.

"I want to take one of the T80s and send it across to the other side of the island with the fourth BRDM, just in case.

Those tanks are old, but the BRDMs wouldn't stand a chance against them in a face to face fight. While they could beat them in ambush with the 30mm guns, I'd feel better with a T80 tagging along."

"Good idea," MacDevitt agreed. "Also, we're going to start shipping the men across the sound to Korotonga tonight by canoe. It should take two nights, maybe three depending on the weather. It looks like calm seas."

"Good. Maxime?" Dan prompted.

"*Oui, mon ami.* Everyone on the ground is now ready and trained. They're keeping low for now. At D-Day plus forty-eight hours, they'll move into their stand-to positions."

"Hopefully we'll get everyone up to speed on the tanks and BRDMs," Dan said.

"*Ja*, we should be able to do that in the time allotted, Captain," Ernst said. "All the men that we're training on them have been handpicked by myself or Maxime."

"I'll trust you."

"A few more things, Captain," Ernst said. "I've spoken to the master of the LST about the pickup of the tanks. All is set for a midnight pickup and a landing on the beach north of the police station at 0300 hours. He also suggested he bring the four BRDMs too, to save time, and also from a safety standpoint. He'll be able to put the tanks and the armored cars right on the beach at the same time and there will be no danger of one of the amphibious cars washing over and sinking in rough seas."

"That will mean that we can't get them to the bridgehead before the tanks."

"Why not? We hold the tanks on the beach, send the one BRDM northbound, send one southbound as recon, the tanks and other two BRDMs backing him up. Either the lead BRDM coming southbound takes out the two Shermans and the Matilda inside the palace compound with its automatic 30mm gun, and continues southbound to its rendezvous with the group of partisans in the south, or engages the tanks with its gun as a diversion, while the T80s come up and engage. Either way, we've got enough firepower to take out two WWII vintage tanks, and that's not even bringing into action the Sagger Antitank missiles," Ernst finished.

Dan was impressed by the men he hadn't chosen who'd been brought before him, and by their tactical expertise.

"That leaves the radio station, afterwards, moving onto the major's rear patio with the heavy mortars," Dan went on.

"Aye, we'll have to assault the radio station. Given the time of day we'll be attacking, 0330, or after the bridgehead is secured in Kotara, we'll place Yasi at the microphone, set up a security detail in case of counterattack, and then me, you, Jimenez, Snodgrass, and Booker make the 500-meter trek through the jungle to the major's house utilizing a path I've cut clandestinely over the last two weeks, and start dropping rounds into the palace compound," MacDevitt stated flatly. "The mortars and ammunition are already pre-placed. Four of the tubes and ammo at the ready and well camouflaged close enough to the major's patio. I'm surprised he's not tripped over them and bashed up his 'gammy leg, eh? Four more are with the north, south, east, and west police units and they will use them in their assaults of the army barracks."

"Everything seems to be falling into place. What about the other BRDMs?" Dan asked.

"They're to rendezvous with the partisans on the north, south, and east sides of the island, lending their firepower to suppressing the soldiers in the barracks located outside those villages."

"Any word on the mine?" Dan probed. He knew the answer, because he came up with the plan. He needed to make sure than all the men in the assault were on the same page.

"We decided to bypass the mine and leave it for last. Taking over the radio station and the presidential palace were to be the priority, secondary was the suppression of the outlying barracks, and when all else is secured, we take the tanks and secure the mine and its prisoners."

"What timeframe we're working under?"

"At 0300, tanks and BRDMs land on the beach. At 0330, we secure bridgehead. At 0400, secure radio station, 0500 secure presidential palace, 0600, we secure the mine."

"What if the BRDMs don't make it to the barracks?"

"It won't matter. They'll be able to suppress the soldiers reacting to the attacks on the palace and radio station."

"Phones?" Dan asked, being thorough.

"Seamus wanted to blow up the interchange box that connected the whole island. I convinced him of the benefits, especially refitting and wiring after the skirmish is over, of cutting the main north, southeast lines."

"Him and his explosives," Dan chortled. "Two weeks as of today. Anything else?"

"Aye. My cousin will be flying in the day after tomorrow. She'll be here for filler, as she called it, and doing some background info on the entire island and people. She'll have a ringside seat to the entire show. The owners of the Grand have reserved her a suite upstairs that overlooks the bridge and approach to the palace. They've also tripled their booze order, and will have beer kiosks where the price will be insanely low. We're hoping that most of the local soldiers will get completely shit-faced drunk and be totally useless by 0300."

"Everyone else will be drinking too, all over the island. Let's make this one independence day they'll truly remember."

"And one that will actually mean something, *non*? Not mere lip-service to an enslaved population."

"I'll drink to that, Maxime," Dan said, holding up his bottle.

"Here, here!" and "Cheers!" were bandied about by everyone.

After the last beer was consumed, Ernst and Maxime said their goodbyes, leaving Dan and MacDevitt alone in the growing twilight.

"What do you think, laddie?"

"I think we're going to pull this off."

"Aye, at what cost?"

"That I don't know, Nev."

"I've found out the details of our Pvt. Hugh Martin."

"Oh?"

"Aye. Left a mother and a sister in Townville, Queensland."

"No wife or kids?"

"No, none of that. It appeared he was putting money away to sail around the world."

"No shit? I'll have to come up with something for his mother and sister. See if your friends can find out if either of them has a mortgage or something."

"Wilco, Cap'n."

"We'll have to find Nguyen San's wife and pay to get her out of Vietnam. Ten will get you twenty the guys holding her in Vietnam have something to do with our Dear Leader Ilikimi's business rivals."

"I was thinking the same thing."

"And now onto the business at hand, Sar' Major."

"And that would be?"

"Why, getting drunk, my good sir!"

CHAPTER 15

The road in front of the Grand Hotel was lined with people, most halfheartedly cheering as each group of people paraded by. The last group of about ten octogenarians carried a faded banner that read: Kiwanis Club International, Korotonga Chapter. Dan wondered if they were going to make it to the palace gate, where the parade finished.

He was also pleased at the way things went after dealing with Nguyen San. The extra soldiers were sent back to their prospective barracks, and the Matilda tank was sent to the motor pool inside the palace compound for a transmission overhaul. The Japanese tank was still outside the radio station, apparently unmanned. The two Shermans, however, were still somewhat of a worry, manned and armed at the north end of the bridge.

Dan and MacDevitt were sitting on the balcony of MacDevitt's cousin's room at the hotel, and had a great view of the festivities. After the Kiwanis Club came the local high school band, trying extremely hard to play Sousa's *Liberty Bell* on key, and failing miserably.

"I hear the fireworks are a go for tonight," MacDevitt commented.

"I've got to hand it to Ilikimi, he throws a hell of a party. Did you see the size of the lovo he had his people put down? There's got to be fifty pigs in the goddamn thing. And the booze! Shit, he's giving it away," Dan said.

"The cops don't appear to be nervous. In fact, they look downright giddy with excitement."

"Let's hope they can curb their enthusiasm until after the festivities, and stick to the schedule," Dan said uneasily. "What's the rest of the day's festivities look like?"

"The parade will finish up at the front gate of the presidential palace at 1800hrs," MacDevitt said, looking at his wristwatch, "which will be in about half an hour. At that time Ilikimi will make his 'State of the Union' address remotely through the radio station."

"He called it that?"

"Aye."

"He's not travelling to the radio station, which was the original plan?"

"Nope. He nixed that right after you killed Nguyen. I don't think he's left his suite inside the palace since."

"That will make our job a lot easier."

"After his speech, the food and the booze will be flowing, and a few local bands will play at two-hour intervals until 0200. Fireworks at full dark, around 2200."

"Cutting it a little close with the party, methinks."

"Aye, there's nothing we can do about it now."

"I need a drink," Dan said, exhaling loudly.

"Have another lemonade, Cap'n."

"I don't want another lemonade, but I will have one," Dan said. MacDevitt reached into a battered aluminum cooler that reminded Dan of the one in his bungalow in Belize, and that sent a wave of sadness washing over him. He didn't want to think about Maria right then.

MacDevitt pulled out a pink and white 12-ounce can and handed it to Dan. "What is this stuff?"

"It's from the States. I ordered it special."

"Too goddamn sweet if you ask me," MacDevitt griped.

"It'll keep us hydrated, and sober."

"I can handle me grog!"

MacDevitt grumbled incoherently and waved to the passing parade, pulled out a pipe, and filled the bowl with tobacco. He struck a wooden match on the heel of his boot and soon had the bowl burning hotly, a cloud of pleasant smelling smoke surrounding his head.

Dan could never understand how cigars and cigarettes, burning the same plant, could smell like shit, and when put in a pipe, and it had the most pleasant aroma. Pondering this, he lit a Marlboro and took a sip of the canned sugar water they called lemonade.

"By the way, I haven't seen Zara all day. It was nice of her to let us use the balcony."

"Och, who knows where she's gotten off to? She took her camera and notepad out with her first thing this morning."

"Not exactly what I was imagining," Dan said, thinking about the petite blonde-haired woman with a Kiwi accent that came up to MacDevitt's waist.

"Aye, I'm not sure what happened to that side of the gene pool in me family. We're all over six foot and ginger, women included."

"She seems nice enough."

"She is. She's keen on this story too. I think she's spent too much time down there in New Zealand reporting on sheep and earthquakes."

"Will you ever tell her the real story?"

"Probably not. I'll let her think it's the ol' MacDevitt luck that landed her a big fat juicy coup d'état in her lap for tomorrow's brunch."

Dan picked up a pair of binoculars and scanned the crowd from left to right.

"See anything?"

"Nah, no four-and-a-half-foot tall blonde dressed in bright pink to be seen anywhere."

"She's probably up near the bandstand, Danny boy. Stop worrying about her, laddie. She's my kin for fuck sake,"

MacDevitt teased good-naturedly. "You're not getting eyes for her are you?"

"While she *is* pleasing to the eye, I'm not the one getting eyes for her. I think ol' Ernst is though."

"You don't say? That's pretty funny. Do you have someone on the side?"

"Sar' Major, I believe that's none of your business, but to be completely truthful, there is a woman in Belize I'd like to think is waiting for me."

"I understand. You keep business and personal life separate. It's the same reason I didn't tell you about my wife here."

"I think you and I both should get some sleep," Dan said, and stood to go into the darkened bedroom.

"Aye. I'll set the alarm for 2100."

The men entered the suite through the French doors. Dan sank down into an overstuffed sofa and was immediately asleep.

>>><<<

After their brief rest, the two men wound through the growing crowd of revelers, across the bridge, past both Sherman tanks, through the main gate of the palace compound, and to their quarters without incident.

They went to their respective rooms and changed into jungle fatigues, web gear, and painted all their exposed skin with light and dark green face paint, taking an AK74 from its hiding place and locked and loaded a 30-round magazine, leaving the chamber empty.

Dan headed out the back door to his rear veranda, where the majority of his men had gathered. They were fifteen minutes ahead of schedule.

"I don't need to take a head count," he whispered. "I assume Maxime and Ernst are on their way to Korotona?"

"Yeah, boss. They headed out by outrigger an hour ago when the fireworks were distracting everyone," Cleatus Snodgrass said.

"Alright. Are we all ready?"

All Dan could see in the darkness was darkened faces and heads nodding assent. He was about to give the order to move out, and was interrupted by a quiet voice from the back of the crowd.

"Eh, Cap'n," Seamus Callaghan said, "if ye don't mind me askin', if our main objective is right here, not twenty yards away, why are we all leaving the compound? Why don't we all stay here and rush the palace?"

"Seamus, we've been over this. We need to take over the radio station and get Taito Yasi on the air. That's the important part. Once we do that, and isolate the compound here, we've as good as won the battle *and* the war."

"If ya say so, Cap'n."

"I do. Any more questions?" Dan asked testily. "If not, shall we get on our way?"

With no more dissention, Booker Davis made secure a fast rope from the rafters of Dan's veranda to the ground twelve feet below. When it was secure, one by one, the men silently slid down the rope like a fireman's pole. Once on the ground, crouched and dashed towards the hidden entrance to the Bougainvillea wall. Dan was the last one down the rope. He took one last look around.

Surely leaving two of the men behind with a heavy machine gun wouldn't be a bad idea…

No. No second guessing. The plan would work the way it stood. Besides, there were political ramifications to consider. They couldn't be seen carrying arms in support of the coup. It had to look as if the police had risen up without help.

He stifled a laugh at the thought of that. Sure, the cops here had no help, those brand-new T80 tanks had washed ashore after the last typhoon. With that thought in his head, he scanned in front of him, and seeing no other obstacles, crouched and ran towards the hole in the bush.

Once inside the canopy of the hollow bougainvillea wall, he saw Archie Davies strapping on a big Soviet pack radio that had been hidden there. He quietly called each unit afield, and all checked in that they were standing at the ready, awaiting the go/no go order from Dan.

"What about the armor?" Dan asked.

"They say that the LST isn't there yet. They've been in contact with the ship, and the captain assures them that he'll be on time."

"Let's move out then," Dan ordered.

The men observed strict noise discipline, even though it probably wasn't necessary with the partying going on only a few hundred meters from where they were slipping into the jungle. They made good time to the rear of the gas station along the road heading east into the jungle and over the mountains, since taking the road wasn't an option.

Coming to the south bank of the Kota River, they waded across the waist-deep slow moving current single file, until all the men were across. Putting Sergeant Lukas Verhayen, a big Belgian who stood over 6'4", on point, the small band of soldiers silently slipped away into the jungle, heading north. The radio station was only a kilometer away, up a steep hill and through thick jungle.

Dan and his men would be lucky to get to their pre-planned assault positions by 0300 hours, when the armor should be on the beach. At 0130 the column stopped, and Dan was requested to come forward.

When he got to the point, he found Lukas with two dozen armed police dressed the same as Dan's men.

"Captain," the policeman in charge said, "the way ahead is clear. We cut a trail through here yesterday up and through the rendezvous point."

"Excellent. Where is Yasi?"

"He is well, hidden away close to the rendezvous."

"Alright then, lead the way," Dan said, and the native policeman slipped back into the jungle.

Booker Davis came up to Dan and whispered, "Cap'n, Archie sent a message. The LST is loaded and will be on the beach to disembark the armor at 0300."

"Well done. Let's get a move on. We've got an hour and twenty minutes to get to the objective."

Booker headed out into the jungle. Dan stood by until everyone was past his position, and he took up tail end Charlie. Not that he feared he was being followed; old habits die hard, and it never hurt to follow procedure.

At 0255 the men reached the objective rendezvous, and rapidly took positions surrounding the radio station. Dan could make out the glowing coal of a lighted cigarette in a sandbagged machine gun emplacement and smiled at the lack of discipline.

Using a pair of Soviet night vision goggles, a gift from Yury, he panned the area left to right, then back again, not seeing more than five other Korotongan troops at the radio station. He let out a sigh of relief.

He called Seamus and Archie Davies over. When the two men were in front of him, he told Archie to give Booker the pack radio, and explained what he needed them to do.

⟫⟪

At exactly 0300 hrs, the prow on the LST shoved onto the reef exactly one mile north of the town of Kotara, halfway between Kotara and the airport.

The clamshell doors opened in the bow, and the hydraulic rams whined to life, lowering the ramp. Even before the ramp was all the way down, Ernst Bauer was already off the lip of the ramp, on the sand and checking the firmness. It was full low tide, and the flats separating the reef from the beach were only covered in a few inches of water, the sand beneath his feet as firm as set concrete.

The big diesel engines on the T80 tanks roared, followed by the smaller, still powerful BRDM engines, the noise deafening compared to the silence of the beach.

Finding the last few yards of the beach near the tree line before the road became unacceptably soft, Ernst motioned for some of the men to come forward with the plywood they'd saved from the crates to place down on the soft sand to allow the heavy vehicles to cross it.

As soon as that task was completed, one by one the four main battle tanks lurched forward, and controlled by inexperienced but enthusiastic crew, sped down the ramp, over the short stretch of lagoon and beach, through a pathway marked by Ernst, and onto the paved road, pivoting south, towards Kotara.

The lead tank stopped and idled in the center of the road, blackout lights dimly illuminating the way south. The driver and commander were waiting for word from Ernst, who was still dealing with the BRDMs coming from the beach, to proceed. The tank commander, a sergeant on the Korotongan police force, prepped and loaded his 14.5mm DShK machine gun that was on a ring mount on his cupola, and ordered the gunner to load a HEAT, or High Explosive Anti-Tank, round in the main gun. He also load the 7.62mm coaxial machine gun and safed both weapons.

After the last BRDM was off the LST, Ernst took a flashlight and sent the bridge three blinks to let them know they were clear. As soon as he had done this, he could hear the ship's engine increase power, and it slowly backed off the beach into the sea, the ramp raising and clamshell doors closing.

The LST and her crew had done well. Now Ernst had a different job. The tail end armored car was pulling off the beach and turning northward when he made it to the road.

After a short discussion with Maxime, the driver, and its crew, it sped off northward to meet up with their fellow rebels on the north end of the island. Maxime followed Ernst until he came to the middle BRDM and climbed inside the cramped confines.

Ernst walked south, stopping at each vehicle and speaking with its crew briefly. They were ready. He got to the first T80 and climbed up on the rear deck, taking a seat on the turret next to the commander, who was standing tall in his cupola, eager to show his tutor he'd learned his lessons well.

"Are you ready?" Ernst asked.

"Yes, Sergeant. We are ready."

"*Gut.* You may proceed. Everyone is ready behind us."

The tank commander spoke briefly into an intercom microphone. The engine revved twice and shot south. Ernst had to hold onto an antenna mount for dear life for a moment until the tank driver settled down to a respectable speed.

They only had one mile to go, so they would be at their objective in a few moments. Ernst looked at his watch; 0317, ahead of schedule. The driver slowed down as they approached the town, and came to a complete stop in the middle of the road across from the tiny primary school. The other vehicles in the formation were spread rearward several hundred yards for safety, and all came to a stop when they could see the brake lights of the vehicle in front.

The tank commander dropped down to look through his thermal sights, and ordered his gunner to do the same. Ernst radioed to Dan that they were in position and ready to secure the bridgehead. When he got an affirmative reply, he radioed the armored cars forward, and told the one that was staying in Kotara to pull up in front of the school and dismount its infantry.

Ernst gave the thumbs-up to the tank commander and dropped down to the ground, trotting over to the BRDM parked near the school. He took five men with him along the side of the road southward, when night became day.

They had gotten as far as the police station, the Grand Hotel between them and the north side of the bridge, when the lead tank's gunner placed the crosshairs of his thermal sight on the turret ring on the old Sherman tank on his left.

The range was only about three hundred meters, and with the huge main gun of the T80, it might as well have been point blank. The HEAT round hit exactly where the gunner aimed, and in a millisecond, molten steel and fragments of the turret shot forward inside the Sherman's hull, killing all five crewmen instantly, and setting off all of the tank's stored 76mm main gun ammunition.

The ensuing explosion shot the Sherman's turret one hundred yards into the early morning sky, where it hovered for a second and fell, spinning rapidly as it did in a straight line, hitting the ground next to the fiercely burning hull with a loud thud.

Even before the turret hit the ground, the southbound BRDM screamed around the T80, and headed across the bridge. Ernst could see the turret on the armored car's roof that held a 14.5mm DShK machine gun fire upon the remaining Sherman tank, green tracers bouncing away in a spray, the heavy 14.5mm rounds from the big machine gun doing nothing but cutting gouges in the armor and waking the crew. Even as the crew reacted to being shot at, the BRDM was already south of the bridge, its turret traversing left and right, searching out targets of opportunity, the Sherman tank left behind in its diesel exhaust.

Sixty seconds had elapsed as the lead T80 tank's autoloader had loaded another HEAT round and fired at the second tank, with similar results as the first. In less than two minutes, the bridgehead was secure and both Sherman tanks had been neutralized.

The first T80 rolled forward, and as it moved past the still burning Sherman, the last BRDM turned left and sped up the mountain road towards the east side of the island, followed by the two remaining T80 tanks Dan had made the decision earlier to send eastward overland to assault and take over the mine.

Ernst could hear the 14.5mm heavy machine gun fire as it sped past the palace gates, no doubt firing up the Bren gun carrier and the guard house. Across the road, from between the post office, doctor's surgery, and the fruit and vegetable market came about a hundred men, all clad in OG107 jungle utilities, and armed with AK74s.

Ernst stood and waved over the company commander of this indigenous unit and was greeted with a wide smile.

"Hell of a sight, eh?" the Korotongan said.

"*Ja.* One hell of a sight."

"Sad to see brothers die. It's also sad to see brothers on the wrong side."

"True. Are you ready?"

"Yes, we are ready," the company commander said.

"Then head out. You've got your orders," Ernst said. He smiled and gave a thumbs-up.

The Korotongan police officer-turned-soldier rallied his men with a whistle, and they split up and took cover between the two tanks and one BRDM, moving cautiously southward across the bridge.

Ernst lifted the handset to the Soviet pack radio that the dismounted Korotongans brought with them and called Dan to give him a sitrep.

⟫⟫⟫⟪⟪⟪

Dan handed back the radio handset to Booker. "Everything is going according to plan at the bridge. Moving across now, destroyed both tanks, and no more resistance since."

"That huge crack and boom must have been our tank engaging theirs. Now what?"

"We wait until Archie and Seamus get back."

"I hope they hurry up."

"We're a half-hour ahead of schedule, brother. No rush."

"I want to get this shit over with."

Booker caught some movement and pointed it out to Dan, who spun and saw Archie Davies and Seamus Callaghan slinking out of the jungle not five feet from where Dan was squatting.

"How'd it go?" Dan asked.

They knelt down beside Dan and Booker. "It went as expected, Cap'n," Archie said.

"Aye, it wasn't pretty," Seamus chimed in, "but it's done."

It was then Dan noticed the blood on both men's blouses, and he understood.

"Alright then, let's go." Dan stood, followed by the rest of the men who were close enough to hear, and walked purposely towards the front door of the radio station, confident that Archie and Seamus had neutralized any threat outside the building.

When he walked around the sandbagged machine gun emplacement he saw the bodies of the crew. No wounds could be seen, though even in the dim moonlight a huge pool of blood at the bottom of the nest glittered, and Dan knew these men hadn't died fast or painlessly.

He reached the door to the building and cracked it open slightly, listening inside. Hearing nothing, he motioned for Booker to come up. "Booker, go and tell all of the men to meet me here, and after you've done that, go get President Yasi and his men into the building."

"I'm on it."

Dan opened the door wide, slung his rifle, and un-holstered his Browning 9mm, cautiously walking down a long, dimly lit corridor. He didn't know if there were more soldiers inside the building or not, and he'd rather be ready if there were.

He went to the end, and saw one red light over a door, and a window in the wall that opened into a small radio studio. There was a Korotongan man at the microphone wearing headphones. He was facing away from the window, so Dan couldn't see his face. He was talking into the microphone, and had put a vinyl album on the turntable.

Dan tried the doorknob, found it unlocked, and opened the door silently. The DJ had finished talking and flipped a switch to turn off his microphone. Dan took two long strides into the cramped studio and placed the muzzle of his pistol up to the back of the man's head.

"Alright, Wolfman Jack, raise both your hands where I can see them."

"A-anything you say, sir," the Korotongan stuttered, his voice shaking.

"Are you the only one here?"

"Yes, everybody went home after the celebrations. I'm the late night DJ."

"Well, late night DJ, you're about to have a special guest, so crank up the power on the transmitter why dontcha?" Dan said with an evil grin.

Two Korotongan partisan soldiers came forth, followed by a diminutive, hunched figure, and when the DJ saw the man's face he broke out into joyous tears.

CHAPTER 16

"*Scheisse!* Shit shit shit!" Ernst shouted, throwing the handset of the pack radio in disgust.

"What is wrong, Ernst?" Maxime said. He'd returned from a round trip through the jungle and had met back up with Ernst on the south side of the bridge. The company of police/soldiers were behind both tanks and the BRDM across the road from the palace, with the ocean to their back.

The Matilda tank was sitting in the middle of the parade ground, between the front gate and the palace, burning brightly like a bonfire. The lead T80 tank had made it all the way to the closed iron gates and was ready to ram it open when the crew of the Matilda fired off a hasty shot from their main gun.

Hasty and wild shot it was, it was also lucky. The British 2 pounder or 40 mm round was a mere mosquito to the T80's 130mm Smoothbore, and the crew fired out of sheer terror at seeing the monster from under the bed at their front door.

The muzzle of the gun was depressed, and the gunner never even used his sights. He pointed it at the behemoth at the gates and prayed. The round left the barrel, hit the macadam halfway to the T80, but didn't explode. It continued on its trajectory, going cleanly between two iron bars before hitting the left track of the T80 with enough force to detonate the tiny amount of nearly 50-year-old cordite explosive. Tiny enough to be barely felt inside the big Soviet tank, big enough the shear the link pin of the left track completely in half. As the driver hit the throttle to ram aside the gate, the track spun off its guide wheels, leaving the lead tank a fifty-ton roadblock.

The fact that the crew had successfully engaged and destroyed the Matilda tank was moot since it now blocked their only egress into the palace compound and the palace army unit was starting to get their shit together.

Already they had five Vickers .303 machine guns on the palace roof, and had set up four more around the parade ground, effectively sealing shut the compound for now. All the attackers could do was to hunker down and wait for Dan to get to the major's house and start dropping mortar rounds on their heads.

They all did what they could, and even the crew in the disabled tank fired the co-ax and main machine gun from time to time at targets of opportunity, reporting back what they could see from their vantage point.

Ernst told Maxime all of this, and let it sink in.

"*Oui*, this is not good. Or as the *capitaine* says, *un-good*."

"I gave him a sitrep. He's not happy, and he's heading to the major's house to man the mortars right now. Good news is that they took the radio station without a casualty, and President Yasi is now on the air, reporting his miraculous resurrection and retaking of the powers of office."

"Now to get out of this mess, *mon ami*."

⤜⤛

"Everything is secure here. We're way ahead of schedule everyplace, except the palace," Dan reported to the men around him outside the radio station. "We're going to have to beat feet down the hill to the major's house and get on those mortars."

"Is it that bad, Cap'n?" Jimenez asked.

"It ain't over. It ain't good either."

"Let's haul ass," Snodgrass said, standing up and tightening his rucksack traps.

The sun was beginning to creep up over the eastern horizon, and even though it would be hours before it reached over the mountains, it was still light enough now to aid the soldiers in their mad dash through a kilometer of jungle to the major's rear garden and patio.

When MacDevitt said that he'd stay behind to make sure there weren't any counterattacks, Dan agreed and the rest began the trek to the major's house. During the run downhill, Dan worried that they could continue the siege until he could get some rounds downrange and that the Korotongan army units still loyal to Ilikimi might try a breakout.

It took a good hour to run the distance through the jungle, and once the band of mercenaries reached the major's house, they quickly dragged out the mortars and ammunition from their cache and set up the four tubes for firing while Dan reestablished communications with Ernst and Maxime down at the palace front gate.

"*Was, was! Was* is all this then?" came a shout from the house. The major, dressed in house shoes and a bathrobe, wielding an ancient double-barreled shotgun was coming right for Dan.

Jimenez and Davis both stopped setting up their mortars and un-slung their rifles, coming up beside Dan.

"You two go back to what you were doing," Dan said calmly.

"What—"

"Do as I told you," Dan cut him off as the major came up and aimed the shotgun at Dan's chest.

"Sir! You are supposed to be an officer and a gentleman!"

"Only by act of Congress, Major," Dan said.

"What makes you think you can come here and take over my patio?"

Ignoring the major, Dan said, "Did I fucking stutter, Jimenez? You and Davis get back with Snodgrass, and start putting some HE on that parade ground."

"Yes sir, Cap'n," Jimenez said, and both he and Davis went back to their mortars.

"I'll ask again, Captain," the major insisted, "what makes you think you can waltz in here and—"

"We didn't waltz, and your patio is a perfect location for our mortars to fire upon the palace compound," Dan said matter-of-factly.

"You mean you lot are performing a coup d'état? From my *patio*?"

"Don't flatter yourself, Major. We've been at this for hours now."

"Why didn't you ask me, Captain Kruger? I could have been of some use…" the major said, letting the shotgun fall out of his grasp. Dan grabbed it before it could hit the ground, and taking the major by the arm, assisted him to a lounge chair. "Ilikimi was a worry and needed to go for quite a while you know, old chap. Yes, yes, he was quite a worry, and a trouble, and needed to go. I could've helped…"

Dan grabbed the radio handset and called Ernst, receiving an immediate reply. It was a stalemate at the front of the palace. If he could get some covering fire on the parade ground, he might be able to get the crew of the disabled tank out and fix the track.

"Ernst, I'm about to start dropping some HE down on them. Forget about the tank. Take half of the infantry you have there and circle around to the north then east, got it?"

"Yes, sir, got it!"

"Do that as soon as the mortar rounds start landing. Give the radio to Maxime to adjust the fire. Get the rest of the infantry, the ones you'll leave there, to bring up all the portable Sagger missiles we have on hand, and start targeting the machine gun nests and the two tanks, and BRDM rake over the palace with main gun rounds and coaxial machinegun rounds. Really pour it onto them."

"And while all that is going on, you want me to take my half through the jungle and through the bougainvillea, round our barracks, and take them from the flank?"

"Exactly. Be sure to let Maxime know when to cease fire."

"Wilco."

As Dan set down the handset, the first mortar round was dropped with a loud *wham!*

⟫⟪

At 5'6", Joey Sutcliff felt slightly cramped in the cockpit of his rebuilt, 'Frankenstein' Mitsubishi A6M Zero. He fired over the radial 1130 horsepower Nakajima 14-cylinder radial engine and it coughed to life in the early morning haze. He let it idle until the temperature gauge was reading in the optimum.

Releasing the brakes, he taxied out onto the runway and down to the west end. This time of day always had an offshore breeze coming from the west. He revved the engine up and down a few times, lit a Lucky Strike, and leaving the canopy open, pushed the throttle to the firewall and released the brakes.

As soon as he did that, the home-built fighter virtually leapt down the runway. Joey barely had to touch the stick and the plane soared into the sky. Retracting the landing gear, he scanned the instrument panel and seeing everything was good to go, climbed slightly higher and leveled off at 2,000 feet, heading south.

He tuned his radio onto the pre-set frequency and depressed the microphone button in the control stick.

"Apache 6, this is Divine Wind 1, how do you copy, over?"

"Good morning, Divine Wind 1," Dan replied, his voice crystal clear over the radio. "We've had a little bit of a setback at location one. If you could, a little aerial message to the parade ground and palace might be what the doctor ordered, over."

"Roger copy that. I'll assume that everything east of the palace gate is unfriendly?"

"For the time being. We're going to infiltrate the compound from the north after a pass from you, over."

"Copy that. ETA is five minutes. Divine Wind 1 out," Joey said, and banked the plane east into the rising sun that was still eclipsed by the mountains. He'd have two, maybe three runs on this vector before he'd need to change to keep the rising sun from blinding him.

Once the plane was on the right heading, he finished his Lucky Strike, flicked it out the canopy, and armed his wing machine guns and cannons. He grinned.

⁂

The BRDM and the two T80s travelling up the narrow jungle trail eastward to reinforce the partisans attacking the east coast army barracks discovered where the other three Sherman tanks were the minute the BRDM crested the mountain by the entrance to the mine.

Someone at the palace must have gotten the word out to the garrison at the mine before the phone lines were cut, because one Sherman tank was blocking the road, 76mm gun pointed right at the BRDM.

The driver of the armored car only had the time to slam on the brakes when the Sherman's main gun fired from the range of two hundred meters, and the gunner's aim was true. The 76mm high velocity antitank round struck the thin frontal armor plates, slicing a huge hole right through the center of the vehicle, a gout of yellow flame belching out of the rear.

The crew never had a chance, and all died instantly. The commander of the T80 behind the now burning BRDM kept his cool, and had the driver inch forward until the gunner could get a sight picture on the Sherman.

The Sherman's crew was fast. They were able to load a second round into the main gun and the gunner placed the crosshairs of the ancient optical sight on the turret of the massive T80 three hundred meters in front of them. Holding his breath, he squeezed the trigger and fired his round, only to see it bounce off the T80's thick army turret, sailing harmlessly into the jungle. They were not able to reload a third round.

The shell that bounced off the T80's turret was harmless, but rang the thick armor on the Soviet tank like a bell. With ringing ears, the gunner placed his sights on the side of the Sherman's hull and pulled the trigger.

At three hundred meters, the sabot on the 130mm round barely fell away when the depleted uranium penetrator round pierced the side of the Sherman using only kinetic energy, and spewed forth molten steel to the entire inside of the tank, killing the crew instantly and setting fire to all of the remaining main gun and coaxial machine gun ammunition. The commander's hatch blew open, and like a roman candle, shot a gout of flame one hundred feet into the air with a popping and cracking sound similar to firecrackers.

He ordered his tank forwards, and with brute force, shoved the burning BRDM and the dead Sherman tank out of the way, long gun tube traversing left and right, searching for more targets.

The rear T80, until then merely a spectator to the battle that lasted barely more than a minute, began to move up behind the leader. When they had reached the entrance to the mine, the lead tank turned left and started to head into the mine complex, only to be greeted by hundreds of Korotongan infantry soldiers setting up several Vickers machine guns.

Harmless to the behemoth, the .303 British rounds from the Vickers sounded like popping corn to the T80's crew. The sound of the rounds hitting only annoyed the crew, and the gunner swiftly hit the switch to change his controls over to the coaxial machine gun.

As the big green tank continued up the trail, the 7.62mm coax machinegun began to fire, sweeping left to right, mowing down the defending soldiers like wheat. Still, they refused to surrender ground and seemed determined to fight.

The police sergeant, now tank commander on the lead T80, looked through his optics at the carnage outside. Although he was disgusted, he never told his gunner to stop firing or the driver to stop. He spied another Sherman tank rounding the sugar cane field, and shouted out a warning. It was too late.

He sat in wonderment as the second Sherman tank erupted in flames, turret launching high into the air from a huge explosion. A jubilant cry in pidgin came over the radio, and he realized the tank behind him had taken out the threat.

Now, to get further into the mine.

※※※

"Roger, we'll keep our heads down, out," Ernst said into the handset, motioning everyone to get down.

They could hear it before they could see it, and all eyes scanned the skies looking for the ancient aircraft. They were under the canopy of the false bougainvillea shrub behind the barracks, and Ernst kept them under cover, because the last thing he wanted to do was have a friendly-fire incident.

He stuck his head slightly through the hidden entrance, and could now see the Japanese Zero, off to the west, first rays of the morning sun glinting off freshly polished Perspex.

And Joey opened up with all guns. Even over the sound of the screaming radial engine, everyone on the ground heard the ripsaw sound of the 7.7mm Japanese machine guns in the wing roots, and the deeper, slower chug, chug, chug of the 20mm cannons in the nose.

In the blink of an eye, the Zero was past, banking north to make another pass, Joey laughing merrily as he gripped the controls.

>>><<<

The Zero passed right over Dan and the mortar crews on the major's patio. Dan saw Joey looking down, grinning ear to ear, and waving. Although the dark green paint had faded away, he could still make out the big red 'meatballs' on the wingtips. The plane banked south, coming around for another run from due west.

Secondary explosions rang out from the compound below, and huge black plumes of smoke rose high into the stratosphere. Dan figured that anyone within a hundred miles could see those plumes by now.

The Zero came in fast again, strafing everything from the front gate to the palace building itself yet again, and smoke was billowing out of some upstairs windows of the palace. Also, their old barracks building was completely engulfed in flames.

After that strafing run, Joey flew south and called on the radio, letting Dan know he had enough ammo for one last run and he'd need to head for home. Dan thanked him and wished him luck.

When he got off the radio with Joey, Maxime called and said the first T80 was repaired and ready to bulldoze through the gate. Dan gave his assent. The sight of everything burning and damn near destroyed around them, the sight of what they once thought was a dead tank in front of them, and now the old airplane coming back for a third time was the limit for most of the Korotongan soldiers under siege in the compound.

Those who were still alive.

A Land Rover, MacDevitt at the wheel, came driving up through the major's garden and stopped next to Dan.

"What's the word, Sar' Major?"

"The word, Cap'n, is the president. Yasi, that is. He is staying in the radio station at my request. The police units north and south report complete success. The crew from the east was heavily engaged and pinned down, holding their own for the time being. Also, the BRDM and the two T80s that headed east report that they were engaged heavily at the mine entrance, and the BRDM was destroyed. Two Shermans also reported destroyed, and are now engaging the infantry guarding the mine with coaxial machineguns."

"Shit. Any more rosy news?"

The Zero screamed overhead so low Dan swore he could count the rivets. Joey wigwagged his wings as he barely cleared the major's roof and disappeared north toward the airport. Dan went to the Land Rover and took the handset of the radio to call Maxime.

"Oui, everything is going swimmingly. Both tanks and the rest of the infantry are inside the compound, and those that aren't dead on the other side are laying down their arms," the Frenchman reported.

"Where's Ernst?"

"I haven't heard from him or the men he took through the north wall of the bougainvillea a while ago."

"We'll have to sort that out later. Fall back to the Grand Hotel for the last part of our plan."

"Oui, Capitaine. Wilco."

Dan tossed the microphone into the Land Rover and along with the rest of the crew, piled into the vehicle for the quick ride down the hill to the hotel.

⫸⫷

Ernst came out of the bougainvillea behind the guard's quarters with the rest of the men and rounded the corner in the lead.

He spied the side of the palace, and looking up through the thick black smoke of the burning tank, spotted several soldiers on the second floor setting up yet another Vickers machine gun. The bottom floor looked totally gutted and was partially on fire, yet somehow the second floor was still intact.

Giving the NCO with him instructions to send the men across the void behind him at fifteen second intervals, Ernst bolted across the open area between his old barracks and the palace itself. Reaching the far wall and cover, he found the door to the staircase leading to the second floor in splinters.

Men began arriving behind him, and breathlessly he started up the darkened stairwell, partisans following behind him. He reached the top of the stairs and cautiously crept to the first room where he thought he saw the soldiers setting up the water cooled machine gun.

Taking a grenade from his belt, he pulled the pin and lobbed it into the void, counting to five. At the end of the count, he was rewarded by a loud blast and the shrieks of the men manning the gun. Flipping the selector to full auto on his AK74, he leaned in and in one sustained burst, emptied the 30-round magazine into the room. Swiftly changing magazines as he entered, he switched back to semi-auto and put a single round into each supine figure, making sure they were dead.

With the men that were now coming up the stairwell behind him, he went from room to room in the second floor of the palace, lobbing grenades and leaving the clean up to the partisans.

By the time he was at the president's private quarters, he was in a state of rage. He kicked the door blocking his way open, to be greeted by the troll Tiki, who was holding a small revolver and looked like he was about to shit his pants.

"We can make a deal!" he squealed in an unnatural, high-pitched voice.

"I'm not interested," Ernst replied and fired a three round burst into the offensive man's chest, knocking him to the floor, where he lay, motionless.

It was then he noticed another form lying on the ground. He went over to the motionless shape on the floor and realized it was Zara's photographer.

"*Och mein got!*" he shouted and bent down to see if the man was alive. He checked his pulse and found he was only unconscious. He saw a set of huge double doors that Tiki had been standing in front of and without hesitation, readied his rifle and kicked them open.

Standing behind a huge desk was President Ilikimi, and held in a headlock was a very frightened Zara Taylor.

"Stand back! I will kill her!"

"You harm a hair on her beautiful head and I will kill you, *Du bist tot,*" Ernst said in a voice as icy as a glacier.

"Ernst! Help me!" she shouted, trying to get free of Ilikimi's grasp. Several of the partisans came into the room behind Ernst, standing at the ready though not sure if they should act or not. One, a sergeant on the police force, took his radio and called Maxime, telling him that they were inside the presidential palace, and that Ilikimi was holding a hostage.

"I can make you richer than you've ever dreamed," Ilikimi pleaded. "Let me go and you'll never have to worry about anything ever again!" he shouted as the renewed sounds of small arms fire erupted outside the presidential chambers.

"I will give you three seconds to release her," Ernst stated gravely, "and then I will kill you."

"Please!" Ilikimi begged. "Listen to me!"

"Zara, *liebhaberin,* close your eyes."

"*Eins...*"

"You don't understand! I can make you richer than kings!"

"*Zwei...*"

"*You* can be a king!"

"*Drei.*"

Faster than anyone could have thought, Ernst dropped his rifle to his side, unholstered a Browning High Power, and put one 9mm round right into Ilikimi's left eye. He was dead before he hit the ground, the crimson mist of bone, blood, and gray matter still settling.

Zara rushed into Ernst's arms and held onto him tightly. They stood like that for a moment, until she looked up at him and asked, "Did you call me *lover?*"

"*Ja*," Ernst said, his face changing to a bright crimson.

"I thought so, you big bloke," she said with a smile and a wink.

>>><<<

Joey Sutcliff was on cloud nine. He'd been turned down for fighters in 1942, and always felt like he'd missed something during the war. Although he loved the C47, he'd always wanted to get behind the stick of a P38, or Corsair, or even better, a P51 Mustang.

At least this one time he knew what it felt like to do some good, not that hauling freight wasn't important. Still smiling as he headed towards the airstrip, he failed to notice a green colored aircraft had sidled up to his Zero.

"*Unidentified, eh. Zero, keep your heading and do not try to evade...*" came over his second radio and it made him jump. He looked to the left, and there, ten feet off his left wing, was a dark green camouflaged Harrier with **MARINES** painted in black on the fuselage, keeping pace with the fighter.

Joey waved, then hit the microphone button. "Hey there! Don't worry, I'm bingo fuel and ammo, going to land on that runway ahead."

"I'll follow you in. That is a Jap Zero, isn't it?" the Marine pilot asked.

"Sure is, I built her up from parts!"

"Well I'll be..."

⫸⫷

The police lieutenant on the eastern coast tasked with subduing the barracks on that side of the island was having a harder time of it.

With only one mortar tube, and the BRDM nowhere to be seen, he was now in a broad daylight slugfest with the Korotongan army. He didn't know that the armored car had been destroyed, and the two tanks that were accompanying it were tied up at the mine, where the soldiers refused to surrender.

One of his men came up under a hail of fire from an entrenched Vickers machine gun, and breathlessly made his report.

"Lieutenant! It was reported to me that there was a large movement of soldiers coming east from the mine!"

"Where are they coming from?"

"Down through the jungle, and apparently, they're trying to come through the cane field to the north."

The lieutenant pondered this for a moment, smiling slightly. He looked around at the men near him, and pointed out to five of his best.

"You five, get some white phosphorous grenades, and come with me."

The six men trudged along the road to the far side of the high sugar cane field. They hunched down, and through the sound of the gunfire at the barracks, could hear the soldiers from the mine running through the cane.

The lieutenant instructed each man to a part of the cane field, creating a box, and when he blew his whistle, they pulled the pins and threw the white phosphorus grenades into the dry and highly flammable cane. Immediately, white smoke billowed, and changed to black and they all could hear the roar of the fire, which grew to such intensity that the sun was blotted out.

The lieutenant smiled as he heard the screams of panic and terror from the soldiers caught in the conflagration.

"Is it over yet, Lieutenant?" one of the men asked.

The shadow of a Chinook helicopter flew low overhead and flared out to land on the road between the ocean and the barracks.

"It is now, I believe," the lieutenant replied. He looked into the burning cane field and shuddered.

⟫⟪

MacDevitt skidded the Land Rover to a stop in front of the Grand Hotel, and everyone piled out and sprinted inside, taking the steps two and three at a time up to the rooms.

While Dan and the rest of his men were making a mad dash down the hotel corridor, Maxime shouted up the stairwell.

"*Capitaine*! Ernst reports that the reporter, Sergeant Major MacDevitt's cousin? She's being held captive in the palace!"

"Shit!"

"Cap'n, I'm on it!" Jimenez shouted and headed back down the stairs. "Everyone else, carry on!"

"Are you sure?" Dan shouted down.

"I'm on it, Cap'n! I'll get word if we need help!" The rest of the men dug into their jungle utility pockets for their room keys and disappeared behind slamming doors. Dan stripped off his clothes, tossed the TA 50 web gear and AK74 on the bed, and even though he desperately needed one, skipped a shower and donned cargo shorts and a loud Hawaiian shirt.

Grabbing a fresh pack of cigarettes and new Ray Bans, he left the room and headed to the bar. He ordered a Miller High Life and went out to the street-facing veranda to meet the rest of the men who had done exactly what he'd done.

"Joey phoned. Said he was escorted to the ground by a harrier," MacDevitt said, coming up to Dan from the bar.

Dan looked up. "And here come the Chinooks." A US Marine Corps CH 47 Chinook helicopter landed near the north end of the bridge, near the still burning Sherman tanks. Several Amtracks came up the main road, and two Super Cobras screamed south.

Dan recognized a face in the crowd of armed-to -the-teeth Marines disembarking from the Chinook and his face broke out into a huge grin. "Ah, Poindexter, you beautiful, beautiful man," Dan said, striding across the road towards the idling helicopter and group of Marines standing around.

"Gentlemen, may I be of assistance?" he said, and they all jumped. When Poindexter saw who it was, he wryly half-smiled.

"Kruger, leave it to you to go overboard."

"What do you mean?"

"T80s? C'mon. Where the hell did you get those?"

"Who's saying *I* got them?"

"Don't play innocent with me. I saw the rest of the shit you procured for this foray."

"Have you had a chance to visit the mine yet, Poindexter?"

A Marine lieutenant colonel spoke up. "Who the fuck are you?"

"Dan Kruger, Colonel. Seriously, have you been to the mine?"

"We were going to go there next," Poindexter replied.

Maxime came running up, pointing to the road leading south to the presidential compound, where Ernst with Zara Taylor.

"Holy shit!" Dan shouted, and ran to the pair who looked like they'd seen better times.

"Cap'n, am I ever glad to see you!" Ernst said.

"What the hell happened? And why was Zara inside the compound?"

"I was in there all night, Dan," Zara said.

"You *what?*"

"Ilikimi invited me for dinner and I jumped at the chance to do an up close and personal story, then things got weird and he wouldn't let me leave."

"Who's this, Kruger?" Poindexter asked.

"This is Zara Taylor, New Zealand citizen and reporter with UPI. This is her photographer," Dan said, winking at Ernst.

"Pleased to meet you, Ms. Taylor," the lieutenant colonel said.

"Poindexter, Colonel, you guys need to go and take a look, a really *good* look at the mine," Dan implored.

"Okay, okay, we'll go," Poindexter said.

"You might want to take Ms. Taylor with you and I'll take care of her photographer here until you get back. Remember, Colonel, the good guys are the ones with the Vietnam era jungle fatigues and toting AK74s, okay? I'd hate to see one of the good guys shot."

"Understood, Mr. Kruger, taken under advisement." Poindexter took Zara by the arm, and the two of them accompanied the Marine lieutenant colonel to the waiting Chinook, followed up the rear ramp by the Marine security detail.

"And Colonel?" Dan shouted into the idling helicopter. "You'd better put every single last hospital corpsman you have on standby, because you're going to need them at the mine!"

As soon as everyone was inside, Dan stepped aside and the engines spun back up to full speed. The helicopter virtually shot into the air, heading east, following the road. Two Amtracks throttled up and screamed up the road, disappearing into the jungle.

"Ernst, what the fuck happened?"

"I did like you ordered, Captain. I took half of the infantry around to the north and east, through the bougainvillea.

When we broke into the compound, rounding the barracks to the east, we saw the palace. The entire first floor was destroyed. We took the stairs to the second floor, where we started clearing it out room by room, with grenades. I got to the presidential chambers and saw Zara, I mean Frau Taylor, with the president. He was armed and..."

"And?"

"And I killed him"

"Ilikimi is dead?"

"*Ja. Ilikimi ist tot.* Jimenez... he came up at the very end. I thought that twat Tiki was dead. We all were high-fiving and playing grab ass and... Shit, I'm so sorry." Tears started to flow from the big German's eyes.

"Tiki wasn't quite dead I take it?" Dan said.

"Das untermench is now."

"Everyone is dead in the palace?"

"*Ja.* No quarter was given, sir."

"Go to the hotel and get yourself cleaned up and changed."

After the German departed, Dan stood there for a few moments, thinking about Hugh Martin, Nguyen San, and now José Jimenez. Had it all been worth it?

The smell of death permeated the entire area, and the stench of burning human flesh wafted through the air, making Dan nauseous. He turned his back to the still burning Sherman tanks, and walked back to the Grand Hotel.

His whole crew was now at a few tables they'd pushed together on the rear veranda of the Grand Hotel. President Taito Yasi had come down from the upper floor's balcony, where he gave yet another speech to a giddy crowd even as the Sherman tanks and most of the presidential palace compound burned.

Alcohol was flowing freely in the establishment and teary-eyed toasts were made to Hugh and José, along with whispered conspiracies to get Nguyen's wife out of Vietnam.

Taito walked up to Dan, and with a surprisingly firm handshake, thanked him profusely.

"What happens now, Mister President?" Dan asked.

"I will set up a new government using your US Constitution as a guide. Though it will take a while, we'll once again be a free people, thanks to you and your men."

Dan handed Taito a business card. "Here, you're going to need this."

"What is this?"

"That is the very late Nete Ilikimi's Swiss bank account details. As soon as you can get an international line out of the country, call this number. You'll be surprised how much money the Republic of Korotonga has."

"It's ill-gained money."

"I wouldn't let that keep you up at night, Mister President. Use that money liberally in infrastructure, schools, and the like. And promote tourism."

"Tourism?"

"Yes. This place is a paradise, and done right, you can have thousands of tourists here a year, dropping hundreds of thousands of dollars. US, Aussie, and Kiwi dollars, more money than you can know what to do with."

"You think that will help?"

"Two of my men, Ernst and Maxime, want to talk to you about it. They want to build a hotel and open a tiki bar right here in Kotara."

President Yasi laughed heartily, then spun when he felt a hand on his shoulder. It was Revu Karalaini, who had arrived from a trip to the mine with Poindexter and the colonel.

"Ah, Revu, what have you to report?"

"Mr. President, Captain Kruger, I have told the Marine colonel what you told me to, that we would accept any medical assistance at the mine to help those that were kept there as slave labor to get back into proper health, that we no longer needed the military assistance, that my police force are more than capable of keeping the peace, and that his Marines have twelve hours to completely remove themselves from the islands. If they wish to come back as tourists, they're more than welcome, but for now, they have to leave as soon as possible."

"I'm sure that the colonel and Poindexter weren't all that happy about that."

"They weren't, Captain Kruger," Revu said with a huge grin that split his face.

"One thing I need to ask, Mr. President, in regards to that card I gave you earlier," Dan said.

"Yes?"

"The matter of three of my men who died..."

"Yes, yes of course. Take what you need to compensate those men's families. I will trust you with whatever amount you decide."

"Thank you, Mr. President."

"No, thank *you*. We will forever be in your debt, Captain Kruger. You and your men," the new president said as two Chinook helicopters flew over the hotel, heading out to sea.

⋙⋘

"Neville, I appreciate you coming along, but this isn't necessary," Dan said.

The pair was picking up a rental car from the Avis counter at the Phoenix Sky Harbor airport.

"Aye, yes it is, laddie. They were my men too."

They went out into the scorching mid-day Arizona sun. The parking lot for the rental cars was covered, so the interior wouldn't be like the surface of the sun.

They found the beige Ford LTD, climbed in, Dan at the wheel, and using a hastily marked map, were soon out of the airport and speeding their way to the address that José Jimenez had put down as his address of record.

Dan knew it was hit or miss that anyone would admit to two white men that Jimenez had once lived at that address in the South Phoenix barrio at all, let alone finding his estranged wife and son.

After a few wrong turns and an hour and a half driving, they located the bungalow on the corner of 67th Avenue and McDowell Road. Dan parked the Ford in front of the tiny house, and both he and MacDevitt could feel hundreds of pairs of eyes on them as they walked up the cement block path to the front door.

Dan rapped on the door, and after a few moments, a stout, dark-skinned Hispanic woman answered the door. Dan explained that he was looking for Señora Jimenez, that he and the big Scotsman were friends of José.

"No son la policía?" the woman asked, still frightened.

Dan gave her his most reassuring smile, and produced a photograph of Dan and José together, drinking beer at the Grand Hotel in Kotara. "No, not the *policía;* we were *amigos."*

"Amigos?"

"Sí. May we come in?"

She smiled and ushered them into a tiny, neatly kept living room. In Spanish, the woman explained that she was José's wife, and that he went away to make them money. She told Dan and MacDevitt that he'd been sending home his entire pay each month for the past two years, and that it had stopped last month.

Dan looked over to Neville as he took the woman's hands in his. He told her, as gently as he could, that José had died a hero, and that he was proud to have served with him. He was also there to give her something to help get her and her child by. He produced an envelope that she opened, wide eyed.

"Tiene usted un niño?" Dan asked.

"Niño? Sí, sí. Juan. He is napping right now, he's only six. This check! I cannot accept so much money!"

"You must," Dan said. "José said your son, Juan, he loves airplanes?"

"*Sí*, that is true."

"Here is also the money for a full scholarship to Embry-Riddle Aeronautical University in Prescott, once he is out of high school."

"Oh, my!"

"Now we must leave. And remember to tell young Juan his father was a proud Marine, and he died a hero."

The men left the house and Jimenez's weeping wife. Neither could tell if they were tears of joy or tears of sadness. They drove in silence back to Sky Harbor, where they checked into the Airport Hilton in separate rooms.

They met up later that evening at the hotel's bar, and sat silently for a while, smoking and drinking scotch. Neville broke the silence finally.

"At least that wasn't as painful as the scene at Hugh's house in Queensland."

"Yeah, that wasn't pretty at all."

"You'd have thought that you pulled the trigger yourself."

"Nev, sometimes I feel like I have."

"You shouldn't, laddie."

"It never gets any easier, Neville."

"This next, eh, message should be a lot easier to deliver, shouldn't it?"

"This one is all mine, Neville. You can sit this one out."

"The cunts lied to me also, laddie. It'd be my pleasure to help you,"

"If we're caught—"

"I'm well aware of the dangers, Dan. Listen, I should have died of hemorrhagic fever in some sub-Saharan Third World shithole years ago, so I'm already living on borrowed time."

"What about your wife back on Korotonga?"

"Och, what did you have to go and inject logic into this? And don't you have a filly back in Belize?"

"As long as you know—"

"The dangers?"

"Yeah," Dan said.

"I'm well aware of the fucking dangers, laddie."

"Alright then, I'll make the plans. Be ready to travel in the morning."

"I'll be ready."

"Have you heard if Archie and Seamus were successful?" Dan asked. They had sent the two men to Vietnam in search of Nguyen's wife a month earlier, and Dan hadn't yet heard anything back.

"Yes, through a mail-drop. I got word that they'd found her, had her fees to the smugglers paid in full, and the last they saw, she was on a boat to the Philippines."

"I wonder if they were Ilikimi's competitors in the heroine business."

"From what I gather from Archie, it was completely dirty and underhanded throughout, so yeah, I'd assume Ilikimi's trade was cutting into the Golden Triangle heroin trade."

"He should've hired some bodyguards..." Dan said, and both men broke out into laughter that was so loud it startled the bartender.

>>><<<

Dan had the taxi driver let him off on the side of the road where the long, narrow jungle trail led to his bungalow on the beach. It seemed like a century ago he'd last traveled this road. After the taxi sped off, he picked up his battered American Tourister suitcase and started down the jungle trail.

It was overgrown, and looked as if it had been a while since a vehicle had come down to his bungalow.

Rounding the last bend, he caught sight of the ramshackle hut. A pleasant, lilting voice was singing a song from long ago.

His jeep was nowhere to be seen, then he remembered he'd left it at Franz's hotel in town.

Stepping up onto the front veranda, El Gato ran to him, and as he rubbed his body over Dan's ankles, meowed loudly.

"*Hola*, El Gato! It's nice to see you too!" He caught sight of Maria, sweeping away some dust off the floor. "Hey there, cutie," he said.

Startled, Maria spun around, and as soon as she caught sight of the big blond man, the look of fear on her face changed to joy.

"Dan!" she squealed, launching herself into his arms.

"I thought you would never come back!"

"I promised, didn't I?"

"*Sí!* You did promise!"

"Are you home for good?"

"Yes, I'm home for good, Maria." He picked her up into his arms, kissed her, and carried her to the hammock.

EPILOGUE

Reuters-Pretoria South Africa – Kidnapped a fortnight ago in broad daylight by eight heavily armed and masked men in front of the Amalgamated Phosphates World Headquarters in downtown Johannesburg, the bodies of two Amalgamated Phosphates executives, Nils Van Die Kaap and Jon Bruhl, were found dismembered and burned last night in a Soweto ghetto rubbish tip. Police officials, speaking anonymously, state that even at this early stage of the investigation, they'd never seen the level of torture inflicted on the two executives, torture that had to have lasted days, if not weeks. No ransom was ever asked, and no known terrorist groups have claimed responsibility.

ABOUT THE AUTHOR

Thomas Wolfenden was born and raised in Philadelphia, Pennsylvania, and is an honorably discharged veteran of the US Army. He's worked in several different jobs throughout his life, spending fifteen years in law enforcement and the private security field. He has worked as an automotive detailer, ambulance driver, a nuclear medicine delivery courier, a dairy barn cleaner, and most recently has worked as a ballast regulator operator, a switchman, conductor, and a locomotive engineer on the railroad. He's travelled extensively throughout the United States and abroad, living in Australia, Fiji, and the Solomon Islands. He's also lived in several states; Pennsylvania, Arizona, West Virginia, Kentucky, Idaho, and Florida being a few. He has written several OP-ED pieces for various local newspapers, and had up until recently kept a political humor blog. He's a Libertarian, Life/Endowment member of the National Rifle Association, and a strong supporter of the 2nd Amendment. This is his third novel, and his fourth published work. He's also the author of two full-length post-apocalyptic action adventure novels, *One Man's Island* and *One Man's War* and the dark, gallows humor police novella *Full Moon Fishtown.* He can be contacted at: lostinwv2005@gmail.com